Disciplining Jane

Disciplining Jane

Jane Eyre

BLUE MOON BOOKS
NEW YORK

Disciplining Jane

Published by
Blue Moon Books
An Imprint of Avalon Publishing Group Incorporated
245 West 17th Street, 11th floor
New York, NY 10011-5300

First Blue Moon Books edition 2001
Second Blue Moon Books edition 2004

ISBN 1-56201-401-3

9 8 7 6 5 4 3 2 1

Printed in the United States of America
Distributed by Publishers Group West

"To pluck the mask from the face of the Pharisee, is not to lift an impious hand to the Crown of Thorns."

Currer Bell

Preface

Jane Eyre was sent to Messrs. Smith, Elder in London in August of 1847 and, printers being less busy than they are today, was published in October of that year. It appeared in three volumes, as "An Autobiography. Edited by Currer Bell."

The story is well known, and deservedly so. What has not always been seen, beneath the author's brave and prescient feminism, is the algolagnic or sadomasochistic element at large throughout the narrative. *Jane Eyre* is profoundly and healthily s-m. It is significant that in Jane's school, Lowood, Charlotte strongly exaggerated the discipline of her model, Cowan Bridge School (the Brontë Society having recently reprinted the 1830 Report of this establishment "for Clergymen's Daughters").

The tale starts with the unpleasant bullying scene by John Reed, proceeds to the red room section (oddly anticipatory of *La Chambre jaune* of Jacques Desroix), and then takes Jane to Lowood where almost the first thing the heroine sees is Helen Burns birched. Prepared for such sights by the maid Bes-

sie's animadversions about girls' school ("a place where young ladies sat in the stocks, wore back-boards"), Jane later becomes a governess and marries Rochester, a classic dominant whose "sternness has a power beyond beauty."

"Am I cruel in my love?" Rochester asks her at the churchdoor before their first, abortive attempt at marriage. At the start of the book, after Jane has turned on tormenting young John Reed, the lady's-maid, Abbot, holds her arms and reproves her for striking "your young master." Jane blurts back, "Master! How is he my master? Am I a servant?" Yet later at Rochester's baronial Thornfield she muses, "It had a master: for my part, I liked it better." She peppers her dialog with this term thereafter, almost gloating to herself when she finally returns to the now blind and maimed Rochester, "I can single out my master's very window."

The semantic of the whole book, however, is shot through with s-m, from the initial use of the British schoolboy term *fagging* (Jane's for John Reed) to the Gothic appellations of severe Lowood mistresses like Scatcherd and Harden ("a woman . . . made up of equal parts of whalebone and iron"). When she returns later in the book to Mrs. Reed's bedroom it is to a room "to which I had so often been summoned for chastisement . . . I looked into a certain corner near, half-expecting to see the slim outline of a once-dreaded switch, which used to lurk there, waiting to leap out imp-like and lace my quivering palm or shrinking neck."

In her poems Charlotte could go still further in this direction, and did; they are accordingly replete with wives or women dominated by semi-tyrannical

men, one of whom (Gilbert) descends to his spouse "like a God." Similarly, in Rochester, whose rudeness Jane adores and who pinches her for caresses, the fictional heroine "could not . . . see God for his creature." Her love for him is "an earnest, religious energy."

We now know that both Brontë sisters played with algolagnic fantasies in their juvenilia. Charlotte's *Angria* imaginings are quite frankly sadomasochistic. The main hero, the Duke of Zamorna, is referred to by adoring females as His Sublimity. The acknowledged expert on these "legends," Fanny Elizabeth Ratchford, has shown us how, with the possible collaboration of her extraordinary brother Branwell, Charlotte fantasized a certain Lady Zenobia Ellrington who seems to storm straight out of the small ads in our underground press ("Dominant Female Seeks . . ."). The name Zenobia is acquired from a brave pagan queen taken chained to Rome by Aurelian; she appears in Sacher-Masoch's novel *The Siren*. Charlotte's young mind turned her into a farrago of passions, subject to "fits of rage in which she shrieks like a wild beast and falls upon her victim hand and foot," with the considerable advantage that she could box as well as any man. As Columbia University's learned Richard Chase was the first to observe, Zenobia was thus both mad Bertha Rochester and the little blue-stocking Jane Eyre rolled into one:

> May not Bertha, Jane seems to ask herself, be a living example of what happens to the woman who gives herself to the Romantic Hero, who in her insane suffragettism tries herself to play the Hero, to be the fleshly vessel of the *élan?*

There is nothing contradictory about the fact that *Jane Eyre* is a brilliant feminist document, long before its day, and its heroine a willing sexual submissive. In this Jane merely doubles for literal political emancipators like Rose Luxemburg to come. Jane is fascinated by Rochester's physicality—his amatory adventures in other countries would today be recounted in undoubtedly repellent detail—and desires to submit to him, yet her rational side revolts. No one of Jane Eyre's intelligence could allow feminine subservience in the political sphere, and it is for this very reason that she so cherishes it in the sexual. "My bride is here," Rochester tells her in the proposal scene, "because my equal is here, and my likeness. Jane, will you marry me?" Later he remarks, "Jane, by-the-by, it was you who made me the offer." She readily admits as much—"Of course, I did."

We may now go further into the tormented fantasy of this extraordinary family, with the discovery in a house not far from Haworth of the papers that follow. We have arranged them in two volumes: those dealing with what was called in the famous novel Lowood School forming the first, those depicting Jane's ultimate conquest of Rochester at Thornfield being relegated to the second.

The authorship of these fragments remains, for the present, tormentingly vague. Were they what Mrs. Gaskell called "the truthful mirror" of Charlotte Brontë's thoughts? Were they, rather, the vile outpourings of her brother Branwell, drinking and doping himself to death beside her? Were they perhaps those of the strange consumptive sister Emily, who the villagers thought a boy and whose own fantasy world of Gondal was ruled by a dominatrix called

Augusta, ruthlessly reducing husbands and lovers and male children to slaves before her. Or did they stream, infected, from the pen of that remarkable "poet," the girls' father, who liked to lecture his daughters on the sexual differences when he wasn't burning their favorite shoes or scribbling insanely upstairs?

Time alone will tell. . . .

Naked under the lights I was set in the triangle, my arms pulled strongly above me. Mr. Rochester stood a pace back and to my left, his sleeves rolled, holding his long ivory cane. I was to be whipped.

It was not for the first time, but my well-fatted buttocks, drawn apart by the posture, quivered like a girl's; these twin praepostors of my whole person knew what they were in for. I had admitted guilt, and was to get it.

"Relax, Jane," he said gently.

Then it came. There was that ritual whirring of air, like the ripping of stretched fabric, then the sense of his slow animal stride completed by a thick meaty rap as the whippy tip connected with my person. I gasped, quickly. Christ, how it hurt. Always worse than expected. I jerked, clenching my cheeks as the livid flame deepened in me. It was going to be a bad one, very bad. The first sweeping stroke had been long and low, and was still chewing into me. One's flesh knew from the first cut what it was going to be like. My thighs quivered as he drew back.

ONE!

It had started.

I shut my eyes and tried to recall it all. My childhood at Gateshead, after my parents had died, school at Lowood, then here . . . with HIM!

1

There was no possibility of taking a walk that day. The cold winter wind had brought with it clouds so somber, and a rain so penetrating, that our usual afternoon exercise was out of the question.

I was glad of it. I never liked long walks, especially on chilly afternoons: dreadful to me was the coming home in the raw twilight, with nipped fingers and toes, and a heart humbled to the region of my high patent leather boots by the comfortable chidings of Bessie, the nurse, and my skin already tingling to anticipation of attentions to my nether person on the part of Abbot, milady's maid, who seldom failed to find some excuse to induce what she called "a more sociable and childlike disposition" in me by application of the rod on return. She knew just how to inflict it most tellingly, too, not merely to make young flesh smart but also my mind conscious of my constant inferiority to Eliza, John, and Georgiana Reed.

The said Eliza, John, and Georgiana were now clustered around the fireplace in the withdrawing room, roasting chestnuts. Mrs. Reed had relinquished her darlings to recline on her bed for a while. She usually arose, dark-eyed, around five. Me, she had dispensed from joining their group, saying she must really exclude me from privileges intended only for contented, happy children.

A morning-room, little visited, lay at one end of the house and I slipped in there, to keep away from their tormentings. "Let's have some fun with Jane" was all too often their favorite game at such moments. The room contained a book-case. I soon possessed myself of a volume and mounted into a window-seat, drawing the red moreen curtain close, so that I was shrined in double retirement. So I remained with Bewick's *History of British Birds,* happy at least in my way, and fearing only interruption. It finally came. The door opened and I heard the poisonous whisper of John Reed.

"Boh! Miss Mope!" He paused, finding the room evidently empty. "Where the dickens is she? Lizzy! Georgy! Jane is not here. Tell Mama she is run out into the rain—bad animal!"

It was well I had drawn the curtain, I was thinking, fervently hoping that John Reed would not discover my hiding-place. Nor would he have himself, for he was not quick either of vision or conception, but Eliza's voice snapped sharply, "She's in the window-seat, to be sure, Jack."

A fleshed feminine arm shot through, two plump fingers clipped an ear-lobe, and I was sent spinning into the room by Eliza, the eldest, my book flying.

"Please," I cried at once. "Leave me alone."

"Leave me alone . . . what?" came the boy's answer.

"Say Master Reed."

"Master Reed," I repeated, nursing an injured ear.

"Come here," he said and, seating himself in an armchair, he intimated by a gesture that I was to approach and stand before him. His sisters stood to

either side of me. Georgiana was grinning, but Eliza's face was baleful. I trembled already.

"Thrash her, Jack!"

John Reed was a schoolboy of seventeen, three years older than I. For, though well filled-out in bosom and bottom, I had but lately turned fourteen. Large and stout for his age, with a dingy and unwholesome skin, thick lineaments in a spacious visage, heavy limbs and large extremities, the lad gorged himself at table and had little love for his younger sister, Georgiana, sixteen, but a perversely precocious adoration for his elder by a year, Eliza.

Me he bullied and punished continually. Every nerve I had feared him, and every morsel of flesh I had on my bones shrank when he came near. There were moments when I was bewildered by the terror he inspired, because I had no appeal whatever against either his menaces or his inflictions; the servants disliked me and would never want to offend their young master by taking my part, while Mrs. Reed was blind and deaf on the subject. She never saw him strike or heard him abuse me, though he did both in her presence—more frequently, however, as now, behind her back.

Habitually obedient to John in order to scape off—for bitter experience had told me he only struck harder resisted—I came up to his chair as he beckoned. To my right stood—towered—Eliza, who at only eighteen was already tall and massive, sensual of face which was usually scowling when directed to me. A dark beauty, she wore her dresses, as now her royal blue wool, close, with little beneath, so that the material moved visibly over her roundnesses when

she walked; at times she seemed to rustle as she stood. By contrast, Georgiana was a very sweet sixteen, cheerful and smiling; her tip-tilted face seemed not to know a care. Her body was all lissom and liquid; under the dove-grey silk she had on now her breasts bulged broadly outwards. I should mention that to remind me continually of my "place" (or lack of it) in this household I alone had to wear short skirts. The plain grey I had on stopped above my knees, where it flared, swirling to my tremblings—"the easier to lift up," as they liked to remind me.

"What were you doing behind the curtain?" asked my male inquisitor.

"Reading."

"Show me the book."

As I went to recover it, Eliza ticked. "Give her a sound swishing, Jack. 'Tis all the little puppy understands."

"She deserves it just for the look in those lovely green eyes, doesn't she just," agreed Georgiana with a chuckle; and while Bewick was being inspected, she chucked me under the chin, saying, "Come, Janey, don't look so cheerful about it. A good hiding won't kill you. It'll only make you want to jump out of your skin a bit. Anyhow, you're getting so fat behind you won't feel a thing." At which her hand roved under my skirt and cupped a knickered chubbie. "Lord, Jack, this b.t.m. is fairly begging for it. What a juicy bum. Do give her a really tight one this time, like you do your fags at school."

"She deserves a sixer for her sneaking way of getting behind curtains," added Eliza swiftly. "Cut her to ribbons, Jack, and make her cry."

"Please," I said unsteadily, crimsoning at Georgi-

ana's feeling fingers.

The boy frowned in his inspection. "You have no business to take our books, you are a dependent; Mama says so; you have no money and no parents; your father left you nothing; you ought to beg, and not to live here with gentleman's children like us, and eat the same meals as we do, and wear clothes at our Mama's expense. Now I'm going to teach you to rummage my book-shelves; for they *are* mine, all the house belongs to me, or will so in a few years. Replace this book"—he tossed it to me—"and then stand out there with your back to us, and lift up your skirt."

While I went to do his bidding, the usual homiletic exchange continued:

"How many are you going to give her, Jackie?"

"Let me position her. She hates it so, bending over."

"She hates it anyhow. But draw it out, Jack. Last time you were far too swift."

"Yes, make her feel it absolutely. Right behind the eyes."

"By George! I feel like Nero. Stiff as a ramrod already."

"Will you stick me after, Jack?" This in Eliza's hiss.

"No! I declare. You're always rogering Lizzy first."

By now I stood facing away from them, and glad to be so, fingers on my hems.

"Get it up," said John Reed.

I hesitated, half-turning. "Please. You don't have to. . . ."

The air sang. Eliza struck strongly. My head

flashed. I tottered and on regaining equilibrium shook it like a dog. Then she left-and-righted me with great welting slaps that bounced my head between her hands like a ball. I gripped my skirt and lifted it high, mewing with pain, half-dazed.

"That's better."

I was at that age. Always inclined to be a rumpy specimen I was conscious of my buttocks from the first. Clad in skintight white batiste knickers, reaching halfway down my thighs, and beribboned there, they were firm and springy without being hard, with a jaunty jut that held them off my back on closely braced white thighs—I was not permitted stockings by Mrs. Reed, a waste of expense. I heard hisses of admiration behind me.

"A ripe pair. Made for whipping, Jack. Drum taut and in prime condition."

"And nicely cleft, with plenty of overhang."

"What a bum! This is better than swishing some cringing fag, ain't it!"

"Pull her knickers tighter, Georgy, do."

Georgy did—so hard that it hurt me in the crotch.

"Yes, I think I can make you feel sorry for yourself, Jane Eyre," said the boy. He stood up. "Now bend down and touch your toes and spread 'em well, and let's take a good look at what we have to deal with here."

I did as bid, striving to keep my thighs together so that the plum of my person would not pouch through and all too aware that indeed it did so, the plump oval at the top of my legs clearly outlined under the thin, almost transparent stuff. I heard Eliza's voice.

"You'd like to stick this into her there, wouldn't you, beast, and make her squeal!"

The boy spoke thickly. "If ever I condescend to take Miss Eyre's cherry I'll bust it so's she feels it through every bit of her belly. If she can walk after it won't be my fault. Listen, Lizzy, if you aren't c-careful. . . ."

"If you make her blub I'll let you put it up my backhole. You know you like it there best."

"It's nice and mushy, eh?"

"I had a pint of cider after breakfast."

I saw them upside down; Eliza had her right arm slung round her brother, her left palm stroking up the boy's big brutal erection, clearly visible up the left side of his thin fawn trousers. It filled me with an increase of sickness and fear. It was a great thick tube whose blunt head gave a demanding jerk against the material as his sister coned it up at the root, then squeezed the ball-bag between the broadly spraddled legs.

"Make her suck it after, Jack, and get it ready for me."

"It's ready for you now."

I gasped. Fingers palped my seam. Georgiana chuckled creamily.

"She's growing fat here, too. And hairy."

"What did you expect," said the brother harshly, "feathers?"

"She was a billiard-ball a year since. You could hardly get a finger in her cunt. Look at it now. The greedy thing."

"Stop it, Liz. If you're not careful, I'll cream." Then to me—"Stand up. That buttock's going to look better for a few lines across it. Get the cane." At the door I caught his snarl—"The long one, mind."

My steps took me through corridors to a flagged passage, giving on an elmy lawn. It was here John Reed kept his things, a racket or two, a cricket bat, and stick. Against a gun case leant two canes.

You devils! I said to myself as I selected the slightly longer and held it like a serpent in my hand. How I should like to break and burn you both! These lithe rods, which the boy brought back from school, were the living instruments of my agony at these perverse children's hands. How I loathed them both!

Each was long, smoothly round, yellow and lean, full of whip and cut, with tips hard as stone—it was there one felt them most, as well my poor sides knew. Each had a small knob-like protrusion to grip one end.

My marrow drained as I held the longer and, I thought, leaner of the pair. It quivered livingly as if all its sleek, soulless length were greedy to get on with the task of cutting into my skin. I made off with it in my hand, head bowed. On my way I met an under-maid, a pretty, pert girl called Olive, who gave me a grin as she went by, plus a roguish wink and much rubbing of herself behind. The staff were happy when little Jane was "for it." How many? my heart was hammering, dear God how many?

Red in the face, John Reed was doing up his trouser buttons when I re-entered. Eliza was licking her lips like a cat after cream, rubbing her hands over one another. Georgiana was busy with an ottoman she had pulled out into the room.

"Here is the cane," I said, as composedly as I could. Experience had taught me that in these cir-

cumstances the best thing was not to get them all excited.

He took off his jacket and rolled up his right shirt-sleeve.

"I'm going to give you six for impertinence. Get over."

"Six is not fair," I said. My heart leapt. I had hoped for less. A "sixer" with that whippy stick could be hell.

"It's what you're going to get," snapped Eliza.

"Across these lovely juicy beauties." I turned at the touch. Pretty Georgiana confronted me, grey eyes twinkling, her simple snub face guilelessly smiling. "Come, Jane," she said, leading me to one end, the familiar one, of the ottoman. "Feeling nice and jellyish inside? I should if I were you. I'm afraid it's going to sting like the dickens. Now then, just take 'em down, Miss Impudent."

I recoiled at this.

"No. You don't have to. . . ."

There was silence. John Reed lashed the air with his rod twice, sickeningly. Then he thudded it eloquently into a chairback. Puffs of dust ensued. I gulped.

"Two extra for keeping on your clothing."

"Please," I asked, near tears now. "It isn't fair. My . . . things are thin and won't protect me at all. . . ."

"Say your knickers."

"My knickers. And, and you can see the marks through. So's to aim. It's not fair to bully me, and use me so, and. . . ."

Eliza seethed. "Make it three more, John. Such modesty in a parson's chit is simple cheek."

"I'll make her sorry with eight, don't worry."

"Eight lovely slices," gloated the grinny Georgiana, sitting on the ottoman and making my hands in hers. "Bend over, Janey."

A smoldering sense of injustice burnt through me as I bent over the settee in the usual position. One arm of it pressed into my thighs in front as, drawn forward by Georgiana's grip, I bent over, legs braced and together, my posterior rounded. She pulled me firmly forward. Georgiana liked to watch my face. Eliza whipped my skirt onto my back and tugged even tighter my bursting knickers. She liked to watch from behind. I felt the measuring tap of the long stick on my skin. All was ready for the fray. Too fast. John Reed went away. I squeezed my eyes tight shut.

Eliza said, "Really hard now. Just over the crease."

There was a long silence. I opened my eyes. Then he came forward at me. The air throbbed with that curious desolating whirr of a whippy cane; this was completed by the meaty thud of impact. My head jerked, I gasped as if flung into icy water, but no more. I was determined not to show them how it hurt. He had laid the rod full across my fattest parts and now stood back as the pain flamed up the whole of my hams, drenching me in its sting.

Georgiana cooed in one ear—"One. Only seven more to go, Janey."

Thhhwulck!

Two. Then three. The bendy whack of the cane into stretched flesh was now echoed by my breathy gasps.

"Lower, Jack," whispered Eliza. "Cut down more now."

Four, five and six were all ferocious strokes, and the last made me jump up and cry out, "Oh no!" Georgiana held my hands, dewy-eyed, smiling.

"Two more," she said huskily.

Then my head buzzed. The accumulation of the cuts began to overcome me and I heard my throat emit a dry whine.

"Bend her over properly, Georgy. I want to come under her well these last two."

"Slice her in two, Jack," urged Eliza.

Whhhhrupp! Red-hot fire lashed my poor soft buttocks and I sprang erect with a cry, tearing my hands from Georgiana's grasp and riveting them to my agonized posteriors.

"Oh . . . oh . . . oh!"

With a rapping crack the cane struck full on my grasping hands, skinning the knuckles of my right. I squealed and danced with the pain.

"Wicked and cruel boy!" I screamed at him, sucking my injured fingers which already bled. "You are like a murderer—you are like a slave-driver—you are like the Roman Emperors!"

I had read Goldsmith's *History of Rome* and had formed my opinion of Nero, Caligula, etc.

"What! what!" he cried, recoiling. "Did you hear that? Run and tell mama, Georgy. But first—"

I ran headlong at him, seized the horrid cane, broke it in two and flung it on the fire, where it blazed amain. I felt him grasp my hair, but he closed with a desperate thing. I raked one cheek with my nails, I do not well know what I did with my hands,

but he called me "Rat! rat!" over and over and bellowed aloud.

Aid was near him. Eliza and Georgiana had run for Mrs. Reed who came quickly upon the scene, followed by Bessie and her personal maid Abbot. We were parted. I heard the words—"What a fury to fly at Master John!" Then in Mrs. Reed's iciest tones, "Hold her arms, Miss Abbot; she's like a mad cat."

"For shame, Miss Jane," cried the lady's maid as she consorted with this order. "What shocking conduct to strike a young gentleman so, your benefactress's son! Your young master."

"Master! How is he my master? Am I a servant?"

"Mama, I'm bleeding like a pig."

They thrust me on a stool where I sat panting, albeit with a pleased eye on John Reed's riven cheek.

"Bessie," said Miss Abbot, "lend me your garters, and I'll tie her hands behind her back." Bessie duly divested a stout leg of the necessary ligature and my wrists were bound behind me. I was losing something of my excitement, and the sheer pain was subsiding. Mrs. Reed approached, and stood over me, a firmly fleshed woman in her forties.

"Wicked ungrateful child," she said at last. "Will you never learn?"

"She needs whipping," said Eliza sulkily.

"Have we anyone here," asked Mrs. Reed laconically, "who can thrash the evil out of this wild cat?"

"Yes, Ma'am," said Abbot shortly.

"Thrash her buttocks soundly, give her an hour of the Red Room and bring her to me when she's contrite."

Phhhhlwupp!

TWO!

I jerked, but did not gasp. The stroke caught me about an inch above the other, but was still very low. With his long steady sweeping drive my master was bringing his cane up under me, bouncing my bottoms like blancmange as he did so. The whip and travel of the rod dug in and burrowed through me.

But the punishment had now started, was on its ineluctable way, its errand of improving my soul by harrowing my flesh. Something in me was called up by womanly pride to show him of my best. I grit my teeth as he drew back. Something in me admired the great lazy strength of his arm which knew so well how to whip.

Then I groaned as a new access of pain swept me from the blow; the basin of my buttocks seemed to spread out in reaction. Make the next one higher, my heart implored, higher, higher. . . .

"Ow!"

2

Bessie and Miss Abbot took me to the top of the house. My spirits were failing me fast as we climbed the wide stairs, plump, comfortable, Scotch Bessie on my left, and hard dour spinsterish Miss Abbot

on the right, the pair of them holding my bound arms as if I were some convict likely to escape.

"You ought to be aware, Miss, the obligations you are under to Mrs. Reed. She keeps you," said Bessie as we went up. "If she were to turn you off, you would have to go to the poor-house for good."

"Please, Bessie," I pleaded. "He was chastising me. He bullies me so. I did not mean to scratch his face."

"You're for it this time and no mistake," was the only grim rejoinder to that.

We had reached the top landing. The floor was little used. But there was one room here. . . .

"What we shall do to you," said Miss Abbot at its door, smiling slightly, "is for your own good." And she ushered me in.

Her words were not new to me, nor was the chamber. It was a high bare room, devoid of furniture but that needed to subdue unruly temperaments like my own. A dim light filtered through unwashed window panes. Abbot turned up the gas. Say your prayers, Miss Eyre, I thought. I was beginning to tremble all over.

"Feeling chilly, dear?" said Bessie, rolling her right sleeve back over. "We'll warm you up all right in here. Strip off now, quick."

Abbot was attending to some pulleys on a wall at the side and Bessie got straps from a cupboard. I, accustomed to such dire preparatives, began to peel off my clothing, all of it.

"Do you leather her first, Bessie," I heard from behind. "Then we'll see how she feels after an hour in the Red Room. I like to work on tender meat."

"I'll tender it up for you right enough, Miss Abbot."

I turned at her touch, nude as a slug before them. They examined John Reed's handiwork on my person with professional zeal.

" 'E fetched her a fair few lively ones, all right, but his aim is all over the shop."

"Work her for me here on the right, Bessie. She's growing up nice and thick through."

"I'll have her blue for you there, Miss A., afore I'm done."

"Please," I whimpered at their inspection, "I'm not a beast, to be used so. I don't deserve to be flogged like this."

Bessie turned me, her face surprised. "Have I ever made ye faint yet, Miss? Have I?"

"How many are you going to give me?"

"Until you're roasted and red as a beet and regretting every second of your little tantrum, Miss."

They took me in their customary way, which was as follows: naked, my ankles and knees were secured with straps. Likewise, my arms at elbows and wrists. Then my arms were hauled up behind me by a hook dangling from the ceiling and adjusted, by Abbot, to a bracket in the wall; the hook raised me and bent me forwards till I hung almost from my wrists.

"Get her right on her toes for me, Miss Abbot."

Bessie took from the wall a heavy tawse. This leathern strap was wide by five inches, thick, and cut into tails at the striking end—where she had thoughtfully hardened them in the fire. The rest was oiled and supple. She stationed herself to my left, swung—and it started. Bessie beat me as she beat her

carpets, with the full force of her brawny Scottish arm. And each stroke whacked into my fat with the sound of a pistol crack, driving the breath from my lungs and making me lurch in my bonds. The curl and lap of the tails on the right was almost unbearable and I was soon hopelessly shouting.

"Yeoww! OW! Oh no. Bessie, please . . . YOW!"

The hard ends fairly belted into me. I had counted perhaps nine or ten when the good woman desisted and the two drew back to survey me from behind, muttering. I was panting with pain. Evidently Miss Abbot gave some instruction as Bessie approached me once more with her strap swinging.

"NAOWWW!"

She gave me three or four more good ones and then they took me down and unfastened me, except as to the arms. I hopped and danced to their delectation for a minute or more.

"Underhand little thing," I heard. "I never saw a girl of her age with so much cover."

"You ought not to think yourself on an equality with the Misses Reed and Master Reed, because Missis kindly allows you to be brought up with them."

"Come, we will put her in the Red Room."

"Pity!" I pleaded, seeing Miss Abbot go to unlock the door.

"One of these days," Bessie said, "God will punish you and strike you dead in the midst of your tantrums, Jane, and where you would go then will be much less pleasant."

Naked, my arms bound behind me, I was thrust

with a single shove through the low door in the wall. I fell forward and I did so, screaming.

The Red Room was a small strange chamber, chill and windowless, with a vaulted ceiling and nothing in it at all. It acquired its name from deep red damask with which the sloping walls had been covered. In this little tabernacle, with no light but a soft blush of pink, I was to be left for an hour, and purchase some indemnity for my fault. Why then, gentle reader, did I cry?

For the correction of the recalcitrant, including the domestic staff, a previous owner had seen fit to pave or carpet the entire floor with sharp wooden pegs. These were such as to make standing up for any time a penance, in truth, and a soft kind of trampling essential. I had fallen on one haunch and side and lay still as a mouse, from experience. The sharp little stakes gradually dug into me with my weight, and Unjust! Unjust! sobbed my reason. After perhaps three minutes, which seemed to be like twenty, the stimulation of the floor pegs became agonizing and to achieve escape from their insupportable oppression I turned on my front. But this was even worse; my breasts begged instant pity. Finally, I contrived to get into a sitting position and then lean back. Though richly wealed my bottoms were still my fleshiest part, and by rolling slowly from one of their pillows to another I managed to endure longer. But at last my heart beat thick, my head grew hot; a sound filled my ears, which I deemed the rushing of wings. Something seemed near me. Steps. I screamed, and screamed again.

The door opened. Light blinded my eyes.

"Miss Eyre, are you ill?" said Bessie.

"What a dreadful noise! it went quite through me!" exclaimed Abbot who was holding some thin twigs.

"Take me out! Let me go!" I pleaded, in tears.

"What for! Are you hurt? Have you seen something?" again demanded Bessie.

"If she had been in pain," declared Abbot, in disgust, "one would have excused it, but she only wanted to bring us here. I know her naughty tricks."

"Out you come, Miss!"

As I crawled out and stood up, tottering, my buttocks felt all bruished and dimpled by the horrid pegs. And already I could see Bessie, this time, busying herself with the pulleys.

"Please," I cried, to the iron Abbot by my side, "I have been punished enough. I promise to be civil. Have pity. Forgive me. I could not," I concluded with a desperate glance at those twigs, "bear another cut."

"You're getting a dozen," said Miss Abbot grimly, "and then we'll hoist ye for half an hour and see if that brings you to your senses, ungrateful girl."

I wailed again. "Not the . . . oh don't hoist me . . . whatever you do . . . pleeease . . .!"

Frantic anguish produced wild sobs. But in vain. This time they hung me straight. My arms secured at wrist and elbow I dangled from the high ceiling pulley, my legs restrapped at knee and ankle. I could just touch the ground with my toes.

"To be so hard to me," I whimpered. "I am only a girl."

"A wild one, and no mistake," said Bessie, tautening a draw-cord.

In this position my rump was thrust ripely back for the rod, its heavy halves braced together and held clenched by me.

Abbot took one withe from her choice, a long thin birch limb of the type I had often, myself, had to make into a rod for her. She stood back and whined it into me.

"Uingh!"

I lurched, losing my footing with the first stroke.

She cut expertly, and the term described her activity entirely. The thin wand of wood sliced into my fatty parts with venom, like a kitchen knife. She worked, as usual, on my underbum but utilizing the bluish bruises left by Bessie. I was soon kicking up my heels like a stranded salmon. Once, after the fifth I think it was, the pain so caught me I swung hissing, doubling my knees up almost to my chest—at which I got such a cut I screamed and jacked my legs down straight, my bottoms juddering. That one had gone right through me like some pure flame. I held it out for the rest stiff as a sentry presenting bunched buttocks for their livid striping. Only my head rolled, and my disobedient tongue fairly barked out short cries, hoarsely. After this they "hoisted" me.

Of all the punishments I endured at Gateshead Hall this was the one my mind most hated; for now that my flesh had smarted, it too was to suffer. I have always had an inordinate dread of heights and what they did to me then, small as it may seem to more fortunate mortals, harassed me quite horribly.

Stout leathern cuffs with rings set in them were strapped about my wrists and ankles, and then the latter swung up to join the former. Working contendedly together, the heartless pair doubled me en-

tirely, head on knees, the hook dangling from the ceiling passing through wrist and ankle rings. Begging and imploring, I was then hauled to its apex and was tethered to its vault, terrified. For if I fell—and for every second of those thirty minutes I would imagine I were just about to drop—I should surely break my back.

"You can cool your sides up there now, Miss."

"Bessie, please. Let me down. You don't know how . . . oh give me more cuts, only please let me down."

They went away, locking the door. I sobbed, dangling, trying not to look downwards, only at the great steel hook holding me, I hoped, so firmly. The minutes ticked inexorably by. I had come to some kind of calm in the center of my panic when I heard a boy's low whisper, from just beyond the door.

"Lizzy! she's nowhere to be seen. They must have hoisted her again. Hurrah! she always hates that."

"It always makes her pee." Georgiana gave a giggle.

"Was it nice and tight, Jane Eyre?" pursued the mocking boy. "Did they scratch your bum a bit more than you did my cheek?"

"Teach! teach! teach!" crowed Eliza's hissing tongue. "You got a juicy dozen. If you ever breathe so much as a word of what we do to you to Mama, I'll see you get two like that, only with her switch."

"Come on, Lizzy. We can't see her. Let's go and have some fun."

They ran off, Georgiana complaining, "Jack, it's my turn. I declare you're always sticking it into Eliza these days."

I sweated as I hung. The minutes passed. I began

to grow crimson. Their suggestion had been explicit. Soon I knew I was going to, I had to . . . I couldn't stop it whatever I did, helplessly hung in this position. It wasn't fair, it wasn't fair. Always this effect on me. With a strangled cry that turned into a torrent of tears the inevitable warm stream frothed from between my flailing thighs and cascaded, in a loud waterfall, on the boarding. I cried softly when it was over.

The key turned stiffly in the lock. I heard their exclamations before I saw them.

"Just look, Miss Abbot. She's weed again."

"The disgusting little thing!"

"And such a copious flow, you'd think she'd been saving up for it a'purpose. Well, she'll have to be reported for that, 'tis sure."

When they let me down I was sobbing but, ah yes, contrite. I lay on one side, my knees drawn up, while they undid my bonds. Suddenly a hand gripped me at the back of the neck and my nose was rubbed into the wetness on the floor, as one might a puppy's. It was rubbed till it felt raw and I squirmed out of Bessie's grasp.

"Troublesome child! Always up to some mischief."

"Let us put this on her, Bessie, and see if she is so free of her hands, after."

The item referred to was a restraint device with which I was uncomfortably familiar. After I had donned my dress, the skirt of which was pinned up high behind, leaving my martyred bottom bare, a leathern belt was fastened tightly round my waist, in the back of which were set two cuffs; in these my little wrists were strapped, one over the other, in a manner to brace my chest forward. No hardened

convict could have been securer. I hated it particularly since it allowed the children their way with me so easily.

Bessie surveyed me from behind, shaking her head.

"Will ye never learn, Jane?"

Abbot contented herself with smacking my face, one, two, three, four times, till my head rang—"Come with me."

She alone led me the long walk to the east wing of the mansion where Mrs. Reed's bedroom lay. Walking behind her I could only be thankful to be spared the taunting of the children, evidently occupied elsewhere. But these for me were awful regions, on which it dismayed me to intrude. I stood trembling before the door as Miss Abbot knocked on it.

"Come in," answered Mrs. Reed's low, almost manly voice and I was pushed forward into the light.

Indeed, there was too much of it for my blinking, tear-dimmed eyes. I could not see past the row of jets, into the darkness of the bedroom beyond. But I could hear.

"Well, Abbot, did you make her sorry?"

"Yes, Ma'am."

"And thoroughly submissive?"

"I'll wager so, Ma'am."

"Turn, Jane. Good, you whipped her well. Now, Miss, are you satisfied with all the trouble you have created? Do you feel like raising your hand to my son again?"

"No, Ma'am."

"Thank Abbot for chastising you."

"Thank you, Miss Abbot, for being so kind as to correct me," I parroted.

"All right, Abbot, you may leave us."

"Beggin' y'r pardon, Ma'am, but she was incontinent."

"What!"

"She weeweed all over the floor."

"Jane, is this true?"

"Yer-yess, Ma'am."

"Disgusting child! Well, I suppose I shall have to deal with that. Thank you, Abbot."

The lady's-maid left. I felt, rather than heard, Mrs. Reed approach behind me. There was a susurration of her silken limbs, a creak of her corseted torso, that was all.

"Excellent. Well wealed on the right, but no skin broken. I'll bet that made you skip a bit, Jane Eyre. Well, that's the last tantrum you throw in this house. I am sending you to school. You are not fit to associate with children of mine."

The pain having abated a little, I longed to retort: They are not fit to associate with me. Instead I got out, as steadily as I could, "I should indeed like to go to school."

A mirthless laugh greeted this comment. "Not this school you will not. If you're thinking of a place where young ladies sit demurely in the stocks, wear backboards, and get a few cuts with the birch about the neck, you are sadly mistaken. I am sending you to a disciplinary academy, to learn some manners. But first, I mean to correct you for your incontinence. Fetch the switch."

After a second I turned and went to a certain corner nearby where stood the slim outline of a dreaded instrument, one with which my sides had been laced until they quivered and shrank with the

pain. My duty was to bring it to Mrs. Reed which I did in the only way I properly could, in my mouth, like a dog.

I saw her now, a buxom, black-haired woman, beautiful but shrewish. She towered over me on shining stiletto heels, her dark gauzy stockings held taut up her thighs by red jeweled garters, and wearing nothing above these but a gleaming corset over a short lace shift. It was in truth too short by far, forming no more than a brief billow at the bottom of the strong spoon of her corset. Mrs. Reed was strongly, closely haired and, as she stood astride, this thick crop above her sex extended under the corset busk. She saw me looking and tscked.

"Impudent child! will nothing cure you? You wait till you get to Lowood. After your first birching there you won't take your eyes off the floor for a week." My eyes implored her as she took the switch. "Now then, let me get at you. Turn about."

"Please, Ma'am. Have pity. May not I be punished another way? I have been thoroughly beat and am completely repentant. It is . . . when they hoist me so, I could never bear it, and I cannot help myself."

"Do you wish to go now?"

Dumbly I nodded.

"Filthy animal. Get it done with then." She fetched a large vase and placed it between my legs. "Hurry, what are you waîting for?"

I strained, blushed, but the only exusions from my person I could produce were more tears. Mrs. Reed crossly removed the receptacle.

"Wasting my time. Turn to the wall, Jane, and lean well forward. I shall be clement this time and

give you but four." As I bent, I thought I heard a sound in another part of the room. "Do you understand?"

"Yes, Ma'am. Only, if you please. . . ."

"What is it now?"

"Please to spare me where Miss Abbot cut. It is so terribly tender there."

"They'll be good licks, low down."

They were. The first sting of the wasp was bearable, just. The second elicited a pant. But the third was a devilish streak of pure white pain, right in the crease. It was more than I could bear and I straightened, hopping.

"Get over, girl. You will have an extra for moving out of place."

As I strove to obey, I heard a growl. A mutter. I went cold and hot all over. A man is here, then. I had never been beat before a stranger in my life.

"Yes, that is right," said Mrs. Reed in evident agreement, "bend further forward, girl, so that I may cut you in there again."

I shivered, waiting.

Thhhhsppp!

"AOW!"

One more. Pray God I could hold out for just one more.

"Jane, you are not bending forward enough. Your body is being punished to save your soul. It is for you to profit from such moments. I intend to give you this last cut as hard as I have ever hit anything in my life."

THHHHSPPP!

"YOW!" I howled, jerking up again and dancing like a dervish.

entry, heavy breathing, steady thumping. The latter was caused by my Aunt Reed's battering on the breast of her pugilistic paramour.

"Dear God . . . so . . . stop . . . ough! No deeper. I feel it in my . . . finish, shoot it into me, come, come, I'm. . . ."

She finished in a forlorn wail and her confederate in a sort of animal snarl. Their contented murmurings then escaped me as I stood, the pain subsiding to a rich warmth in my lower person.

Then, "You don't fuck a woman, you impale her," I heard Mrs. Reed say. Followed by, "I may depend upon this child being received as a pupil at Lowood?"

He laughed shortly. "Madam, you may. She shall be placed in that nursery of chosen plants—and I trust she will show herself grateful for the inestimable privilege of her election."

Some minutes then passed in silence, interrupted by sighs, protests, the sounds of clothing resumed or rebuttoned. After a while I was aware of Mrs. Reed touching me at the shoulder. She looked soiled and sweaty, and thoroughly satisfied. Her bush hair glistened slickly. She turned me and I looked up at—a black pillar! Such at least appeared to me the straight shape standing erect on the rug, in his trousers and shirt sleeves. The grim face at the top was like a carved mask, placed above the shaft by way of capital.

"The Reverend Broughton Brocklehurst," said Mrs. Reed.

"Your name, girl?"

"Jane Eyre, sir."

"Well, Jane Eyre, and are you a good child?"

Mrs. Reed answered for me with an ironic twist of her mouth: "The state of her nether person speaks for itself, I fear, Mr. Brocklehurst."

"Come here, closer," he beckoned. I stepped to the rug and he bent from the perpendicular. What a face he had, what a nose, and what a mouth! "No sight more salutory than that of a naughty child with well-whipped buttocks. You have just been flogged, Miss Eyre?"

"Yes, sir."

"And did you enjoy it?"

"No, sir."

"It hurt, I hope?"

"Very much, sir."

"So that the next time you are tempted to throw a temper tantrum at your betters, you will reflect, will you not?" I said nothing and he went on. "Come now," he coaxed, "confess that the next time you wish to hit and strike a better you will hesitate, for your flesh will know that it will be even more strictly chastised. Admit it now, Miss Eyre."

The term *better* for John Reed was what galled. I dropped my eyes and said, "I suppose so."

The man chuckled. "This is a delightfully mutinous spirit, even with its hands bound behind it. I shall warn Miss Temple to tell her mistresses. They will take pleasure in breaking Jane Eyre in, especially as she is so richly fleshed."

"She shall go to bed without supper and spend the night confined as she is, and if she is no better in the morning I shall deal with her as I never have before."

"So you admit, Jane Eyre, that corporal correction is effective?"

"If it is fair, sir," I replied.

"It is always fair at Lowood," he thundered sternly to that, evidently incensed by my answer, "and every girl is always in the wrong there. The school that I direct, and to which your benefactress is having the kindness to send you, is founded on corporeal correction for young ladies. You will be thrashed and thrashed again, Miss Eyre. You will go in daily, hourly dread of chastisement during your first quarter for, though you are above the age for such, I shall give instructions that you will join the lowest class, the most punished. The superintendent and her staff enjoy whipping nasty, deceitful girls; and they can do it to the letter. You will receive canings across those plump buttocks of yours that will make your eyes start out. And before you have left you will be birched to the blood. You will feel the switch, strap and, yes, the whalebone which cuts like a razor into a girl's soft flesh. There will be days, Miss Eyre, when you'll wish you had not been born with a bottom; you will sob your heart out simply waiting in a corridor or cold room. Yes, you will learn about punishment at Lowood, child; even if I abolished cane, whip and strap there tomorrow, there are instruments a-plenty to test the fortitude of the most rebellious, like yourself."

"Do they still use those stools that you showed me, for Detention? Ugh! I should hate to sit on one of those for a minute."

"Unfortunately a culprit seldom does so for less than fifteen, but I admit I have never seen a look of great joy in the face of one so embedded."

"It must make you want to go, after."

"I should not want to be in the shoes of one who did so, however. No, control of sphincter muscle and

urinary tract alike are taught. Matron takes care of that. After the latter training Jane Eyre here would never have known her little accident just now."

"So you see, Jane," said Mrs. Reed, "you are really lucky. You will be admitted to Lowood school and trained there until eighteen years of age or more. After which they will put you out to earn your living, as a teacher or a governess or custodian of some sort. I shall not care to see you again. In fact, the only time I enjoy looking into your face is when it is crying after a whipping, as now."

" 'Twill be her normal expression for the first quarter at Lowood, I do assure you," comforted Mr. Brocklehurst. His large features were pressed and prim. "You have a wicked heart. You must pray to God to change it by correcting your flesh."

"Only, stay out of sight of Mr. Bricklehurst's great cane, child. What a rod. It makes you faint to look at. Why he is so sharp with the tip he could cut a fly in two with it."

Mr. Brocklehurst seemed pleased by the praise. His big head nodded, smiling. "Got another brace from Tom Arnold at Rugby, only t'other day, my dear. They do say they're being quite universally adopted in the boys' schools now. After all, Keate and Busby, at Eton and Westminster, respectively, were taking such a large part of each day in their birchings. With a cane you come quicker to the remedy, if perhaps a trifle less artistically. Anyhow, Arnold wanted to hurt his boys more and has perfected a fine instrument. You will be pleased to know that in my last visit of inspection to Lowood I tested it on a senior girl, a great big buttocky thing of nigh on nineteen who had been reported to me for re-

peated sloth. I made her recite ten of the Psalms, which she did entirely without error, and then I gave her ten of the best. I am proud to say she got to seven almost without wincing, but by the time it was over it was all she could do not to roll on the floor. I placed well. Her right cheek was a single weal. She had to hobble from the room."

I began to feel faint. Slinging her arm around the man's waist, Mrs. Reed continued triumphantly, "I'll bet she didn't want to sit down soon after that."

"Smelling salts soon restored her. No, I don't see any good in the discrimination of sexes. What is good for a boy is good for a girl. Consistency, madam, is the first of Christian duties; and it has been observed in every arrangement connected with the establishment of Lowood: plain fare, simple attire, unsophisticated accommodations, hardy and active habits; such is the order of the day in the house and its inhabitants."

"Quite right, sir."

I began to cry.

"Ah, that is how I like to see her," crowed Mrs. Reed.

"Do you say your prayers night and morning?" continued my interrogator.

"Y-yes, sir," I blubbered.

"Read your Bible?"

"Sometimes."

"Each new girl, on entry to Lowood, is given a little book entitled *The Child's Guide*. For her first day she is locked up with it and must get its contents by heart; for it contains all the rules and regulations of the establishment, and its knowledge precludes excuses thereafter—when and how to curtsey, to

prostrate before the headmistress, comportment in Hall, and so forth. First thing every morning of her first week, excluding Sunday, a new girl receives three strokes from her dormitory monitor. Not much, but a reminder to go to bed with, that the first thing she will be conscious of when awakening is . . . impending pain. In your case, since you are so buxom, I shall give orders that you are to have three last thing at night before retiring, too. Thus you will be assured by the end of that week of three dozen on your bottom. Count into that a few cuts in this class and that, more if you are so foolish as to incur a demerit, and you will go like a mouse into your second week.

"And now go like a mouse to your room," said the strong-limbed woman beside him, whose fondlings were becoming keener, "and stay there. Bessie will put you to bed."

I curtseyed and backed to the door, whose handle I could only open, like that of my bedroom a minute later, from behind me, my hands being so fettered. I lay on my bed and cried.

Bessie was in not long after, scolding and fussing. She undid my restraint-belt, made me naked entirely, and hauled me to the wash-stand where she inflicted a merciless scrub with cold water and a coarse towel on my face and person and then disciplined my head with a bristly brush. The news of my going to Lowood seemed to have got abroad quickly for as she busied herself about me Bessie dilated on it.

"Ye won't half catch it there, Miss Jane, and no mistake. They'll be always after you, there. Now if you had a nice sore bottom like this, for instance, the mistresses would not leave it at that. Ah no. They

would try to catch and trip you in another fault, so as to have the pleasure of whipping into already tender flesh."

With which consolatory theory she made me lie face down on my bed. She put the restraint-belt on again and fastened my hands behind in its cuffs.

"Not so tight, Bessie, please. Uff, I can barely breathe. No, you don't have to do that . . . please . . . who said? Did Aunt Reed. . . ."

For the good woman had widely parted my legs and was engaged in strapping both to the extremities of the foot of my bed

"There, that'll stop you turning over, and twisting, and playing with yourself like I know you do."

"What happens if I want to . . . ?"

"Ye'll just have to contain yourself this night, my pet. Don't you think you did enough up there just now? I've seen a stallion piss out less. Now then, I have to get to the kitchen. Madam has persuaded Mr. Brocklehurst stay the night, and he is partial to roast onions."

As also to other morsels, I should have liked to add as the servant left me. She left me to pillow my head to darkness and dreams. But neither came. Something else came to me, as I lay.

Thhhrrrwwppp!

THREE!

Slapping into my limpened, spreading flesh the stroke forced a strangled grunt from my throat. It was another wounding cut, and for a second I made the triangle clink with my clenchings.

These first three cuts had laid the basis for the whipping which I now knew was going to be terrifically severe.

3

They came like thieves of my dreams in the night. Georgiana slipped into the darkened room first, and had reached my bedside ere I was aware of it. Like me, she could in her thin slippers walk the matted floor as softly as a cat. The other two glided in straight behind her, Eliza soundlessly closing the door.

"Get her, Georgy!"

"Nooo—!"

My cry was cut off in Georgiana's giggle as she kirtled up her skirts and in one leap straddled my head. Yes, she sat on my nape with her small nervous buttocks, squeezing me breathlessly into the pillow. I gurgled and struggled. In vain. I was held with my legs apart at their mercy, my hands fettered behind. With one of hers Georgiana reached under me,

grabbed my bush-hair and elevated my pelvis. Eliza and the boy lost no time behind.

"Get it right up for me again, Lizzy, quick."

"I'd have thought you needed no help from me. Just looking at those stripes ought to do it to you. Gad, they limed her nicely. She'll carry those switch marks for a week. Mother laid on neatly. There, what did I say, it's kicking like a mule, Jack."

"Now grease it for me."

"She doesn't deserve it."

"I'll never get it in, else. Just look, her bum-hole's no bigger than a thimble."

Suddenly I felt the swing of his humid tube against me, under a buttock. I stiffened out and squealed without making a sound, or accomplishing anything except total loss of breath.

"Hey, help me hold her, Lizzy. She's fighting like a hell-cat."

"I'll settle that. Take your hand away a second."

I felt a great blow in my side, driving what breath I had out of me. I knelt limp, gasping, half-suffocated, as the boy had his way with me.

With his loathsome hands on each of my welted bottoms he puckered open, prying with his thumbs, the anal dimple, his favorite lodging place. I could not even tense slightly, so exhausted was I, and he secured purchase at once. I felt the rotten ridge of his corona slip past the sphincter ring, more of him squeezed into me, moved up and down and—no more, no more, my bursting entrails begged. Suddenly his whole foul length lunged and slucked into me. I grunted with my entire being.

"Now bugger her, Jack. Don't spare her, split her in two."

"Plug her to the hilt each time, Jack," laughed Georgiana in unison. "Go right through her now."

"She's so . . . . damn . . . tight!"

As he began to slide in and out, the coursing girth of his greased piston started to fill me to the gills. I was engorged with the penis of this disgusting boy. I could not breathe. I sweated, fisting my fingers at my back, cursing and sobbing in turn. Fortunately he was generally quick.

"Bugger the shit out of her!"

"I'm . . . going to come . . . pretty damn soon, y'know."

"Hold out, Jack, hold out. She's not felt a thing yet."

Eliza reached under me and taking a nipple between each finger and thumb twisted them as if I had no feeling there at all. A dry whine escaped my throat, and a derisive fart from Georgiana followed. The boy barreled into me, buggering in earnest now.

"Come on," he panted, "try and shit me out. At the end. You know how to do it."

"Squirt it into her, Jack."

"Pump her so full she'll drip for days, go on."

Georgiana managed my thighs completely perpendicular to the bed now as the last thrusts began. I was doubled in two and the glib gristle seemed to be pounding at my ribs as, with an anguished cry, he held still, then jetted into my rectum, falling forward over me.

"Good," said Eliza, standing up quietly. "Clean it on her face before you use the towel, Jack."

The foul boy did so. I collapsed forward, sobbing hysterically, too weak even to vomit. I felt totally used and abused, my poor dilated arsehole oozing.

"Perhaps that'll teach you," said Eliza, "to think yourself our equal, Jane Eyre."

They left me, then. But Georgiana came back. She was chuckling creamily.

"I've come back to give you a goodnight kiss," she said.

But it was my nether cheeks she fondled. Suddenly I stiffened.

"Georgiana, *please!*"

A cold greasy cylinder had slid up my unsuspecting rectum.

"There. Perhaps that will console you for your buggering."

"Oh please. I shall have to go, you know I shall. And no one will come. And I cannot get to the commode like this. Oh please, free my feet."

She left the room, still tittering. I lay and cried my eyes out.

The first cramps started ten minutes later. There is nothing more degrading for a human being than being made to soil herself, helpless. I withstood the pangs as long as I might, and even called for help. But the inevitable overtook me. And I sobbed again.

Cold and dirtied as I was, I must have been exhausted by my struggles of the evening, for I fell asleep. I awoke to hear voices, dimly. The door of the room was ajar. Light lanced in, and I could hear Mrs. Reed and her maid talking.

I heard the former tsck crossly, in her way, and say sharply, "Not again!"

"Yes'm. And you should see her towel. She's a filthy slut, and no mistake."

"Well, I suppose I shall have to thrash her again, and this time properly. What a nuisance the girl is,

to be sure, and how glad I shall be to be rid of her."

"I will go in and clean her up a little first, Ma'am."

"And I shall get my switch." It was said grimly. "Abbot, you agree that 'tis in the best interest of these girls to be merciless to them?"

"I do, Ma'am."

"Jane Eyre has simply not been punished enough."

"I wager she'll be punished enow at Lowood, Ma'am." That, too, was said grimly. And Miss Abbot came in to my room, while the mistress of the house sought out her switch to punish me.

Wh-wh-whrupp!

FOUR!

Oh atrocious!

"Ow!" I cried loudly.

Despite my braced position the cut made my buttocks bound and I lurched in my bonds, groaning. Mr. Rochester examined his handiwork; as always, he had formed the base for a regal flogging. A purple band of pure agony now stretched across my hinds. He palped the weal on the right, where it had swelled thick as a finger.

"Are you feeling it, Jane?" he asked solicitously.

"Y-yes, sir," I answered hectically.

"You are cutting nicely today. I think I'm going to enjoy this dozen."

And he drew back to continue it. I shut my eyes and clenched my teeth. I did not clench my bum. . . .

4

My reward, if such it may be called, came the next morning. After second breakfast, at which John Reed had gorged himself with chops as usual, I was sent to assist Eliza in a long withdrawing-room in which there was a piano. I was to turn the sheets of her music while she practiced, and did so, standing "close enough so that I can pinch your well-wealed bottom for you if you get it wrong."

After a while John came in and Eliza went to talk to him at the other end of the room. Neither molested me. The presence of the Reverend Brocklehurst in the house had cast a distinctly subdued veil over these children.

Suddenly Georgiana burst in, walking fast, in a charming gown of dove-grey velvet, close-fitting, and with a white lace collar. She appeared distraught, and clasping her hands strode hastily up and down. Eliza looked up.

"What on earth's wrong, Georgy?"

"I'm to be whipped."

"Good heavens, what for?"

"Oh after John had stuffed Jane like that last night I went back and gave her a suppository. She spurted all over the sheets, it seems. Mama was furious. Not about Jane, of course, but she said I'd come close to spoiling some good sheets."

"So it was all that wretched Jane Eyre's fault again," said Eliza, advancing menacingly on me. I recoiled. In the state my bottom was in the touch of my clothing was oppressive.

But Georgiana shook her head. "Oh Jane got it again for incontinence, I'm glad to say, but she didn't peach. Abbot found the end of the suppository she'd voided in her writhings and reported it to mother."

Eliza thought. "But Georgy, you must have known of this last night?"

"Oh I thought it would simply be the usual from mother. You know, beastly, but bearable." She paused. "A few minutes ago I learnt that Mr. Brocklehurst has charged himself with the execution."

There was a shocked hush in the room.

"No!" gasped Eliza.

"Brocklehurst is . . . tight," John Reed got out in awe, his jaw slacking.

"Of course he is," cried Georgiana wildly, resuming her frantic pacings up and down, head ducked and face ghost-like. "He's severity personified. That man could make a stone squirm. Oh God, I'll never bear it. I don't know what I'm going to do. He'll cut me in two," she concluded on a sob.

The three of us watched this extremity of apprehension with an awe mingled with fascination. Indeed, a light had come into Eliza's dark eyes, I saw. The poor Georgiana continued to walk up and down, putting her knuckles to her mouth and once feeling behind her, cupping her willowy buttocks as if testing their resiliency to bear the rod.

"Dear God, I'm going to get it. You remember when Mama let us watch him giving it to Molly in the under-pantry. Why, you could have put a ruler over the marks after. Heavens, I shall never bear it, never."

"Georgy," said Eliza in a new tone, and with a thin smile on her lips, "do you have no clothing on underneath that gown?"

"None. Mama said not. The easier to ready myself for the rod."

"What exactly is he going to take to you, do you know?"

"Oh how should I know? That man could make a slipper sting like the fires of Hades." And in a sudden access of broken sobbing she collapsed into a chair, head in hands, crying. The bowed, humble line of her neck and back looked very penitent, indeed. My own throat went dry for her.

"Come on," said John, nudging his older sister, "it's not going to last for ever."

Georgiana looked up directly at me, her tear-stricken face frowning.

"Oh Jane, you don't know what a whipping is till you've had one from Brocklehurst. He doesn't simply flog your flesh, he beats your mind. He . . . completely dominates you, body and mind. Stripping in front of him is even an ordeal. Mama says one fuck from him's worthy twenty from any other man. Feels as if a whole brass band's been through her, cymbals and all. And he cuts so damnably cleverly, just where it hurts most and when the pain's at its worst. With six . . . and it can't be more nor six . . . he'll. . ."

With a little startled cry, half-gulp half-yelp, she sprang to her feet, ashen-faced. A step had sounded, and the creak of a well-oiled boot. We froze as one, really frightened. And when Mr. Brocklehurst strode in, we three mere girls dropped curtseys like soldiers. The man looked well-fed, warm, cheerful and strong, his whiskers much in evidence.

He drew short as he saw us then, smiling, slowly approached Georgiana who stood with hung head to one side.

"Well, Miss, you know why I am here?"

"Yes, sir."

"Ready to take your medicine?"

"Y-yes, sir."

"Your mother has asked me to whip you. Thrash your buttocks. I shall endeavor to give her satisfaction. John," he said, without turning, "I understand you have a cane."

"Yes, sir."

"Fetch it."

John bolted from the room as if hoping to win some hundred-yard sprint. Mr. Brocklehurst continued to bend his bushy brows on his unfortunate victim. He was truly an impressive sight, and thoroughly relishing his role.

"Not been caned by me before, I believe."

Georgiana made a mumble. She was beginning to look extremely fearful, indeed, and it was clear that for her the punishment had started.

Eliza smiled. "She still has the pleasure to come, I fear, sir."

Mr. Brocklehurst gave her a baleful stare and Eliza's smile dropped like a stone.

"That remark was not intended to be impertinent, was it, Miss?"

"No sir," Eliza answered hastily, turning suddenly ashen also.

"I scarcely think our young friend here looks to be anticipating a . . . pleasure. Hh? A little slender and loose-fleshed but still nice and round behind. I enjoy flogging into such a buttock. They generally cut well. No, I shall contrive to make you feel it, Miss."

With a breathless rush John Reed burst back into the room, proffering his yellow rod.

"The cane, sir."

Mr. Brocklehurst took the knob end. With pursed lips he bent it strongly double and then flayed the air with it twice. I jumped and Georgiana gave a despairingly audible gulp. The pitch of the whine the man made was ten times higher than that extracted by John Reed, even at his strongest.

"Too light," the oppressor opined. "Too light by

far to do real work with. Besides, children of your age should have graduated to the cord by now. Yes, a length of well-waxed whipcord is what I should like to apply to this young lady's lower person. However, it'll have to do. I shall make it sting."

"I . . . I used to have another, sir. It wasn't quite so bendy. Only, Jane Eyre broke it."

"Miss Eyre will be considerably less spirited after a year at Lowood School, where she will go next term and where girls pay for their temper tantrums on the block. Yes, Miss," he said, turning his pale eyes upon me, "bare arse on the block, before the whole school. A few licky dozen about the bottom part of it and you'll be howling your heart out. Those mistresses know how to get every ounce out of a cut, they're not employed by me, else. Now then, John, how do you say I should take our unhappy-looking sinner?"

"Take her, sir?"

"Posture, boy. How d'ye get it at school?"

"Bent tight, sir."

Mr. Brocklehurst smiled. "Don't you think it might offend the sensibilities of such a well-brought-up maiden as your younger sister to bend her bottom double before a stranger and expose herself so?"

"I der-dunno, sir."

"Shall we see?"

The man turned upon his victim who was now quite limp and faint. With a quiver of his cane he indicated a very low embroidered stool before the grate.

"Stand there." Georgiana did so. "Now uncover. Uncover for us entirely." The girl looked back, plainly not gathering his drift. The man advanced,

hissing angrily—"Hoist up your skirts, you silly little fool." And he lashed the air again.

With a sob of panic Georgiana ducked and did as bid.

"Right up under your armpits now."

She was, as she had told us, nude beneath the velvet, but for stockings held taut by jewelled garters. Her very white skin had a delicate marbly sheen and her sweet, small, well-set buttocks (trembling already, alas) looked utterly defenseless as they huddled together under our inspection. Mr. Brocklehurst jounced the right hind gently with the tip of his stick and it gave a muscleless wobble.

"Strange to think that this young lady," he said reflectively, "is in a few minutes going to look as if she's sat on a grille, and rather harder on the right than on the left. John, this is tender meat. 'Twill cut like butter, too. I fear she'll feel it. Bend over and touch your toes, girl, now."

Georgiana dipped like a hinge, her dress slipping up her. Her charming, sly buttocks tightened till they appeared as twin lengthenings of her thighs which, however, were still pretty plump at the top—not enough so, though, to prevent the plum of her person from pouching back. Mr. Brocklehurst gave us all time for a lengthy contemplation, in total silence, of Georgiana's divided person, and its thickly furzed sexual slot. I felt very sorry for her, indeed.

Finally, he said on a growl, "Does that make you come hard, eh, Jack?"

"Yer-yes, sir."

Mr. Brocklehurst guffawed. "I'll wager it does, you rascal. And I'll bet you'd be spurting to see me lick into those cubs, eh? But I have another idea for

you after, boy. I like to make the punishment fit the crime. Now, Miss, lean further and put your palms absolutely on the carpet in front of you. Right down, mind. Brace your legs." As Georgiana strove to obey, she widened still further behind. Her knees bent. "Can't do it with yer knees straight, girl? Come on, try."

"I'm trying, sir."

"Well, try harder. Push back. If a Lowood gel can't put her palms on the ground with her knees absolutely stiff after a year, she gets exercises in a special stretching apparatus . . . daily. Now, what is this part of your anatomy I am touching the tip of my stick to?"

"Sir! Please."

"Its name, child."

"Anus, sir."

"Good." He turned to Eliza, "Synonym?"

"Arsehole, sir."

"Good again. She'll be wanting to use it shortly, with a pint of castor oil in her entrails. Now then, Miss, stand up straight, here. Well, I declare. We seem to have restored some color to the upper cheeks, to be sure."

Indeed, when Georgiana straightened, her hems falling into place again, the tint of her face was a beetroot hue, in strong comparison with her upper arms and bosom.

"With a thin-skinned seat like yours, Miss, I don't need ye fully bent. Lean forward a little, so. A trifle more for the material to adhere behind. Now put your hands behind your head. Just so. I will take you so, with the fat relaxed. You will hold that position on pain of extra cuts. Now then, what do you

say to a salty six? 'Twill take no more than a minute."

"Yer-yes, sir." The crystal of a tear stood in Georgiana's eye nearest me.

Mr. Brocklehurst swept her a courtly bow.

"Come, take your deserts."

He led her briskly to the far door which gave onto a passage and a door across into a little-used study. As it closed on Georgiana I thought she looked very small.

"By Jove, he's a tartar," whispered John Reed.

"He's going to hurt Georgy," said Eliza.

"Heavens, he put it to her. What a bum!"

"I hope he slices it in little pieces," said Eliza slowly and joyfully, closing her shining eyes and pressing her clasped palms into her lower stomach. John Reed's fist was in his flies. The complicity of excitement, against one of their own, on the part of these depraved children shocked me quite utterly. In the long silence that ensued I heard Eliza breathing thickly.

"Grit your teeth, Georgy!"

Suddenly a quick sharp *snip* came to us from beyond the far door. Muffled, it made no more sound than might a snapped twig, in that anxious air, but I believe we all three startled perceptibly.

"One," said Eliza softly, pressing at her lap.

There was another similar rap, and she said, "Two."

My own palms felt damp. Georgiana was finally suffering and I was familiar with that cane's sharp sting. There was a good long pause after three, for Mr. Brocklehurst knew how to draw it out, and an even longer one after four. After she had counted it,

in fact, Eliza murmured, "Getting warm, I fear."

Then a fifth was given, followed by what might have been a stifled cry, followed by a low growl. Then Eliza was saying, "Six. Damn," and straightening her skirt. John Reed hastily did up his trousers which did not conceal in the slightest the gluttonous tube of gristle up one side of them. We stared at each other.

Suddenly a harder rap resounded. We blinked, and its fellow followed after. Shortly after that someone appeared to be wrestling with the door-handle.

Georgiana shot out, closing the door behind her, red in the face and panting, "Oh, oh, oh." She curled over, holding her bottoms and mewing like a kitten as she came past us. It was a very salutory sight indeed to see her hands grasping her velvet-clad chubbies in great bunches.

"Excruciating," she gasped out. "He didn't have to hit me that hard. The man might have been cutting a tree-trunk in two. Whew! And he didn't even strip me."

Bursting into tears, her face contorted, she positively writhed her way from the room to—no doubt —hers.

A moment later Mr. Brocklehurst emerged and came into the room, humming. He was easing his left arm back into his jacket and restored his cane to John with his right.

"Not bad at all. I think I stung the little sinner. She writhed nicely at the end. We believe in justice, and equality of the sexes. Now then, Jack," he said, with a meaningful look at the boy's apparent erection, "at school, do you bugger your fags after you've swished them?"

"Sometimes, sir."

"Good boy. When you're hard up, like now, I reckon."

"Yes, sir." The scratched cheek grinned.

"And we understand, your mother and I, that is, from Miss Georgiana last night, that you buggered Jane Eyre here."

John Reed paled, uncertain. "Yes, sir," he said.

"Fine, fine. I hope it was a nice slick tunnel."

"It was, sir," he got out with relief. How I hated the brute, then.

"Excellent. You show promise, boy. Jane Eyre," slowly the pillar revolved towards me, "did you feel well and truly stuck up the entrails by this likely lad?"

"Yes, sir," I said. And it was beastly true. I had.

"Good again. Now then, as I say, we are just. We believe in fitting the punishment to the crime. Miss Georgiana is now drinking a pint of castor oil, after which she will be secured on her bed just as Jane here was. John, m'boy, I want you to go up to her and when the infusion seems to be beginning its work, and the little lady is nicely squirming, I order you to bugger her soundly, as you've never buggered anyone before—to the back of her brain, d'ye understand!"

"Yes, sir." His great slow grin was loathsome.

"Feel up to it?"

"Yes, sir. Thank you, sir."

"Don't spare her now. Time it right and 'twill give you the sensation of your life."

"I won't, sir!" Once more he dashed off, happily waving his cane.

Slowly, yet more slowly, Mr. Brocklehurst gyrated towards the other spectator of the scene—Eliza, who had stood with slightly open jaw, a rabbit mesmerized by a snake, albeit a fleshy one.

The Reverend Brocklehurst summed her with his most basilisk gaze, and approached behind her. Eliza made no move as he placed his large hands on the top of her bottoms and then drew them down, over the protruding surfaces, finally cupping one healthy hind in his palm and jogging it meditatively.

"By heaven, this is a base I should like to operate on. Made for the birch. First-class meat, in prime condition. So thick through, yet springy. What d'ye say, Miss Eliza, would you care for me to put it to you?"

"I don't think I should like it at all, sir," the girl replied weakly.

"Think I could make these heavy hams of yours twist and writhe nicely?"

"I am sure that you could, sir."

"Well," said Mr. Brocklehurst with relish, standing back to survey her again, "before I leave I shall ask your mother to summon me for the next infliction of which she deems you necessary. George! I'd come from the other ends of England to whip into such a sumptuous seat."

There was a little silence, then, frowning, Eliza said something odd. "I would feel proud if you would, sir."

Mr. Brocklehurst's great mouth grinned.

"What!"

"Yes, sir," she continued, breathing heavily, "I know it would hurt abominably and though I should try not, I should probably screech and struggle, but

to have been whipped once by a master of your caliber, sir, would do honor to my sex."

"Three dozen with a briny birch, Miss, bent over."

"I shall be ready for them, sir."

"And for the last cuts, I shall whip in."

"I am sure you will," the girl said huskily.

With an ironic smile the Reverend bowed and left us.

Eliza turned dazed eyes to mine. She seemed half in a dream. "What is it, Jane?" she said in the same lost tone. "That man, why he whips you as he looks at you. I don't envy you going to Lowood."

"I shall be quit of here," I said sullenly.

"Jane, I nearly always come when I hear Georgy beat by mother. Sometimes twice. But this time I was too frightened, it was strange. The power he holds over your mind, it is truly frightening. Now he's gone I feel like spending. Come into this window-seat, quick, and get under my skirt."

"Oh all right," I said, even more disagreeably.

In a second I was buried in her thick coarse muff, which I was forced to service with my tongue. The sooner it was over the better for me. The heavy girl mashed herself into me, bucking her hips on the edge of the seat, and pulling my head into her. It was fortunately soon done. With a hoarse cry of "Oh Christ!" she liberally bedewed my lips and face, spasming richly. Then there were footsteps and she kicked me from her. When Bessie came into the room I was wiping my face on the back of an arm and Eliza was lolling a leg with feigned unconcern in front of the fire.

"Miss Jane! You naughty little thing! Why don't you come when you are called?"

"Because I didn't hear you," I ventured. But she was not angry and as she led me kitchenwards I put an arm through hers with youthful lightness of heart. "Come, Bessie, don't scold."

The action was frank and fearless and somehow it seemed to please her.

"Ye're a strange child, Jane. I shall miss you when you go to school. Come and help me peel some onions."

"It makes me cry."

"And not the only thing as does, eh?"

"Do you like whipping into me, Bessie?"

"You sharp little thing! You won't be so venturesome and hardy after a year at Lowood."

So I helped her with the onions and rejoined the rest for luncheon. Mrs. Reed came down on the arm of the Rev. Brocklehurst looking as if the brass band had been through her and back, cymbals and all. John Reed was there, looking grinny and complacent, and Georgiana was there, looking closely at the carpet.

"Portrait of a well-caned girl," laughed her mother. "Show your marks, Georgiana."

The girl had to do so before us all. She still had nothing on, beneath, and the man had properly grilled her. He had covered the whole limp buttock, each stroke a half inch exactly below its peer, purple bands against the white. At the very base, just on the fold, was a very solid weal indeed.

"Those were the two extra," he told us, indicating. "I'll wager they were the worst, were they not, Miss?"

"The very worst, sir," promptly admitted Georgiana.

"Good Lord, sir," said Mrs. Reed, shakily pouring

a bumper of sherry, "and you were able to effect such nicety of placement through clothing?"

"She moved once, after one cut, which made me go awry . . . here." He indicated again. "But I think she was sorry, after. I should dearly like to try my skill, such as it is, on your elder, Ma'am."

During lunch Georgiana said not a word. Eliza continued to look at the man as though mesmerized, and I kept counsel with myself. I could still feel my whipping under me.

About the time port wine was circulating Mr. Brocklehurst and Mrs. Reed were looking tolerably flushed. He put aside his great glazed napkin, pushed back his chair and opined, "A fine repast, Ma'am, in truth. But this morning's work has given me an appetite for more whipping."

"You are incorrigible," said Mrs. Reed.

One by one, we asked to be excused.

Before he left that afternoon, however, a maid was found who was guilty of some peccadillo. Mr. Brocklehurst was saddling up in the stables. The girl was a poor slim under-housemaid, who had to stand shivering for ten minutes in the cobbled court before he was ready. She then had to strip completely and in public, before the grinning stable-boys, on the back of the stoutest of whom she was subsequently horsed or hoisted. Mrs. Reed lent her thin switch for the occasion and the man gave her a dozen. Though she kicked amain the cuts all came within an inch or so, and the skin was broken in two places on the right side.

All this was told me later. I was below-stairs aiding Bessie at the time. The three children watched the infliction from an upstairs window, and I simply

saw the girl moaning and sobbing in the main kitchen later. Despite Bessie's stories of Lowood I looked on my coming schooling as a blessing. I would be glad to be quit of Gateshead and told her as much. Even for me life seemed to have a gleam of sunshine.

Thrrrr-wupp!

FIVE!

"Aaah!"

Merciful Heaven! The stroke went right through me. The cut was fiendishly low and full of whip. My buttocks quivered like jellies and I felt them slipping together with my sweat as I clenched them in my agony.

He had taken me cleverly on a previous welt and the pain seemed to mount and mount unbearably. There was a good solid lump now under my bum on the right. I felt a pure panic that he should continue to work there.

I rolled my head convulsively round. "Please, sir," I panted, "it's burning so. Oh but please cut up at me higher. You are slicing me in two . . . like a razor. Oooooh!"

At the same time I strove not to unclench. I saw him watching, biding his time till I slackened, and spread, when he would hit once more into the fatty, relaxed flesh.

Dear God! I closed my eyes, trying to pick up courage from those early days at Lowood. . . .

5

Five o'clock had hardly struck on the morning of the 19th of January, when Bessie brought a candle into

my room and found me already up and neatly dressed. I was to leave by a coach which passed the lodge gates at 6 a.m.

Bessie was the only person yet risen and as we passed through the hall and went out at the front door, "Goodbye hateful Gateshead," said I.

"Oh, Miss Jane! Don't say so."

"Why not? What have I known here but knocks?"

"You were rather put upon, that's certain. However, I shouldn't like to be in your shoes, where you are going now."

The moon was set, and it was very dark. Bessie carried a lantern, whose light glanced on wet steps and gravel road soddened by a recent thaw. Raw and chill was the winter morning; my teeth chattered as I hastened down the drive. There was a light in the porter's lodge; when we reached it, we found the porter's wife just kindling her fire; my trunk, which had been carried down the evening before, stood corded at the door. It wanted but a few minutes of six, and shortly after that hour had struck, the distant roll of wheels announced the coming coach. I went to the door and watched its lamps approach rapidly through the gloom.

"Is she going by herself?" asked the porter's wife.

"Yes."

"And how far is it?"

"Fifty miles."

The coach drew up. There it was at the gates with its four horses and its top laden with passengers. The guard and coachman urged haste. My trunk was hoisted up, my own destination given. There was some merriment then, since my box was set beside a large bundle of shiny canes, on the same errand.

"The new batch for Lowood, special made from London," said the grinning guard. Bessie clung to me with kisses and then I was whirled away into the unknown.

I remember but little of that journey. I only know that we appeared to travel over hundreds of miles of road. We passed through several towns. The coach stopped, the horses were taken out. The passengers went into an inn for dinner. Once more the guard stowed me away in the coach, sounded his hollow horn and away we rattled.

The afteroon came on wet and misty. As it waned into dusk I dropped asleep. The sudden cessation of motion awoke me. The coach door was open and a person like a servant was standing at it. I saw her face in the light of the lamps.

"Is there a girl called Jane Eyre here? And a bundle of new canes?"

"Yes, yes."

Amid more laughter canes, trunks, and my poor self, stiff with long sitting, were all handed down. Rain, wind, and darkness filled the air. I discerned a stone wall, spiked with gaffs at the top, and a door open in it. A tablet bore this inscription:

"Lowood Institution. Built by Naomi Brocklehurst, of Brocklehurst Hall, in this county. 'Let your light so shine before men that they may see your good works, and glorify your Father which is in heaven.' St. Matt. v. 16."

I passed in with my new guide, who locked the door behind us. There was now visible a house or houses—for the building spread far—with many windows, and lights burning in some. We went up a broad pebbly path, splashing wet, and were admitted

at a door. I was led through many passages to a large room with a fire, at which I warmed my numb fingers. The hearth light showed me a sort of kitchen, with mahogany furniture and shining copper pans.

By its light, and that of some candles, I saw several fresh, pretty faces smiling at me. They were maidservants, I surmised, all in their twenties, mostly black-haired, and made up so highly their faces seemed as if lacquered. At first I supposed this to be the lighting, but it was not. They grinned at me across a wide refectory table.

"She looks tired."

"And hungry too, no doubt. Let her have some supper before Neil takes her off."

"Is this the first time you have left your parents to come to school, girl?"

"I have no parents," I said.

Ravenously did I eat the good, piquant food set before me, my back warmed by the ruddy fire. As my spirits returned, my eyes cleared and I glanced at the lively figures moving about beyond. To my astonishment I saw that their uniform of impeccably fitting black satin, close on the body, concluded well above the knee. They had tiny lawn aprons and caps, and their smoky stockings were taut as sausage casings. Their heels of glacé kid were sheer stilettos. They were a glossy, merry bunch and I heard them undoing the canes and slicing them through the air as I ate.

"These new ones are beauties."

"And look at the tips."

Another juicy whistle made me blink.

"Scatcherd will love that!"

Did they really need so many, I wondered dumbly;

and as I did so, a laughing servant brought in two more bundles from without. A girl approached me.

"Were you caned where you came from?"

"Sometimes."

"These are only what are here called classroom canes, used every day. They are very thin and sting atrociously, but they don't bruise badly. The Duty canes are altogether other, they take all the breath out of you at once."

They looked longer and leaner and suppler than John Reed's variety, and my skin sensed their sting already. Just then a big heavy blonde woman, of about twenty-nine, strode in, and the maids quieted deferentially.

"Was that the last of the new-knicks to arrive?" she asked.

"Yes, she's at table, eating, Neil."

The newcomer came and stood before me, hands on her massive hips. She was bizarrely attired and of a type to inspire both awe and admiration. Her thick flaxen hair was drawn tightly off her broad pellucid brow and collected in a long stiff plait behind. She had a Germanic face and was entirely clad in black leather which creaked as she moved. There was a very short elbow-length black cape, what appeared to be a tightly laced corselet, a skirt yet shorter than that of the maids just reaching to gleaming black boots, wrinkleless at thigh.

"Is your name Joan Eyre?"

"Yes, Miss." I added, "Only it's Jane Eyre."

"You must call me Neil. You call all mistresses Miss and the head Ma'am, but you call us maids by our first name. I am the Head Maid." Perhaps her eyes saw mine look somewhat apprehensively at the

long black switch which I now discerned clipped to her belt at the right, for she smiled and went on, "Don't worry. You will never be punished by me. No Lowood girl is chastised by a maid, but we help in the administration of correction and can report you for such, if you are uncivil to us. We try to see that each new girl gets as much such correction as possible her first quarter here. For her own sake. Are you finished your meal, then?"

"I don't think I want any more at present, thank you," I said.

"Then come with me."

She led me out, strongly striding so that I had almost to run to keep up with her. Her splendid back caught the occasional lights as she led me down long indefatigable corridors and up stone steps to a far wing of the house. Here was a dormitory, dimly lit, with a blackboard outside and one tenant within, already abed. I was introduced to a tiny dark girl of perhaps twelve called Joan Walker, another "new-knick" like myself.

I should explain that the four new girls for the quarter had been, as custom dictated, convened a week before the true start of term and the arrival of the rest of the school. Only a few mistresses were present when we arrived. It was a period of preparation and training, during which we were exonerated from all discipline, and the last day of it, as Mr. Brocklehurst had predicted, was spent locked up with the school rules.

The next day dawned fine and clear and during a large breakfast in the deserted Great Hall my hopes began to rise. Besides Joan Walker, there were Susan Cuningham and Estella Moore, a girl with mousy

hair and a rather plain face yet almost as big as me. We were to learn the building every nook and cranny, and to be tested on our sense of locality, too. Our orientation was in the capable hands of Neil, the Head Maid, who looked, if anything, even more spectacular than before.

Particularly impressive was the Long Chamber, at whose mention matrons in after-life were known to turn pale, an immense hall with a fireplace either side, chandeliers pendent from the ceiling, and a dais at one end. It was also, of course, empty. We were told by our sumptuous cicerone that it was a gathering place, where the Head made addresses, and that no girl was ever allowed to speak in it, without first being spoken to. Neil led us to a large black block, some three feet high, a little way before the dais. It was liberally supplied with straps and a little ledge in front. Somehow none of us had to be told that it was an implement of punishment.

"This is where," our guide told us impassively, "for more serious offenses girls are publicly birched. You will be whipped here without quarter, for it is rare that a girl can go through Lowood without bending over this block a few times. It's usually two or three dozen with a long rod of five or six well-pickled withes, which are then bound with wire. We don't believe in clemency, I fear. You kneel here," she pointed to the ledge and then demonstrated for us, kneeling on it. "And bend forward, so," and she leant over the transverse sloping ledge, her short skirt hiking until the bottoms of taut black leather knickers showed. We four stared, bemused. The great strapping thighs, in their bursting boots, parted slightly. "Legs together, or apart. And sometimes

even feet back, so. You'll get it bare-bum with plenty of time. An order of four dozen can be drawn out by a clever mistress, like Miss Scatcherd, over fifteen minutes, with the girl writhing like a cut worm all that time." Neil stood up. Perhaps catching something in our eyes she added with a casual smile, "You won't see me thrashed, if that's what you're thinking. I keep the maids in order, with this." She tapped her switch. "I'm responsible to Miss Temple directly. If anything is amiss I get far more severely flogged than any mere girl." She turned haughtily, then added, "but I do enjoy seeing you whipped. If I ever have to secure a girl for correction, believe me, by the time I've finished she can't so much as twitch her clit."

It was a dismayed little troop that then followed their mentor round the classrooms. These were bare and utilitarian, each desk provided with stocks, backboards in evidence, and also racks of canes on one wall or another. There was a zeal to punish in evidence, all right. We witnessed it that evening. Our rounds were concluded with a visit to a typical mistress' private chambers, cheerful enough, and then to a typical Chastisement Chamber nearby, as such was called, and this was the opposite of cheerful, being provided with straps, canes, switches, benches and bolts, enough to bring a regiment to order.

Finally, our guide tapped on the large oak door at the foot of some stairs. We were ushered into the large comfortable mistress' common-room. Here two young laughing women, both clad in amazingly brief pleated skirts of a soft tartan stuff, and close black sweaters, were practising swipes with what were evidently some of the new canes sent up.

They looked at us and smiled, but paid no other attention, as we came in. Neil whispered "Curtsey," and we dropped our knees like soldiers on parade. The two mistresses continued their work, or play, which they seemed to enjoy very much. They now took turns in selecting canes and whacking them into the upright of a stout leathern-covered chair, producing puffs of dust and indentations in the material. Each took about two lively paces and, skirt swinging around ample hips, thudded the whippy stick into the stuff with all her might. Before it bounced back the cane in hand would be a liquid yellow flash, joined by a desolatingly deep swish of separated air.

I think we four all gulped. I know I did. My heart was in my boots. Such intensity of concentration, such nicety of aim, such furious velocity of stroke . . . it was far far sharper than that of "Master" John Reed.

The maid said, pointing to the shorter of the pair, a red-headed woman, "That is Miss Smith. She is Scottish. The other is Miss Miller. She teaches Math. Miss Smith is very strict."

After a while more of this edifying spectacle the taller of the two, Miss Miller, strolled over to us. She was a buxom and splendid-looking brunette, with downy dark brows, rather low, and blue eyes; the pleats of her skirt trembled at the top of her voluptuous thighs and the cane in her hand quivered and shivered livingly. But she herself was smiling and cheerful, as she confronted our cheerless rank.

"Are these the four new-knicks, Neil?"

"Yes, Miss. I'm showing them round."

Miss Miller looked Estella up and down with a

roguish smile. "You're so rumpy you'll scarcely feel a thing. Which one is the twice three?"

"Eyre, Miss. Here. Three morning *and* night," Neil pronounced primly.

The mistress stood by me and put a hand under my skirt, cupping and squeezing a hinder cheek. "Mnn. Lovely. I can hardly wait." I thought she gave me a wink as she went, and altogether I had a distinct sensation this mistress liked me. I should get on well with her. Despite the menace of personal chastisement there was a cheerful womanly complicity I sensed already at Lowood, and I felt far from the brutal male world of Gateshead. At least I should not be buggered here.

We curtseyed and left the room. Outside it Neil addressed us with a frown:

"There is one room you will not see, until you enter it for punishment. That is so that the effect shall be greater. The Duty Room is below and you will enter it only and always for punishment. All Demerits are paid off there on the day of commission. There are fifty-five girls at Lowood school this term, eight of them monitors and praepostors. There is no head girl here. The rest are divided into three classes, by virtue of seniority: Major, Minor, and Minimus. You will graduate into the third of these after a month. When a Minimus, or Minnie, as she is called, incurs a Demerit, she pins a badge with her fault on it on her breast for the rest of the day and receives three cuts with a Duty cane that evening. A Minor gets four. A Major five. You may not think three cuts very much, but with the Duty cane it is all you want. I shall show you some of these tomorrow and you will help wax or size them. They are strong,

heavy canes, yet with plenty of whip since extremely long. Mr. Brocklehurst orders them especially and they leave weals as thick as your fingers. Moreover, don't forget that a Minnie incurs more Demerits than her seniors, as a rule, sometimes three or four in a single day, so that the extent of her continual fear can be imagined. You could not possibly take more than four with a Duty and remain still, so that all girls are well secured over the board for a flogging with it. No, I'm afraid there's nothing for it when you enter the Duty Room but to get it into your heads that you're going to suffer severely."

With this admonition we were dismissed for the day. The next was spent putting up birches and waxing canes and oiling straps and leathern tawses. The birches were especially bloodthirsty implements, consisting of five or so (they were graded) thin limbs, toughly budded, culled from the grounds and then latticed with thin wire by our hands. We were told the latter grazed unbearably and that a mistress always "drew" (i.e. blood) after a dozen. If the skin was well flitched on the right, a lotion was painted on which helped it heal but stung insufferably for a time.

This day too, we were minutely measured, in a room at the top of the house. The Matron, a Mrs. Harden, had not arrived, but this was her office. Not only was every centimeter of our outward person chronicled in a book, but the dimensions of every orifice—yes, even the length of our nostrils—also. This was done by a glove stretcher, and it hurt. Hymens were pronounced all still whole, to much merry tittering by the maids. Then we bent over for a sort of cylinder to be inserted up the anus; this was then

enlarged in some manner, to check the dilation of the entrail. Thanks to John Reed's attentions I took this without fuss, but Joan Walker screamed and had to be held. Finally, each pubis was shaven clean. Joan had almost no hair, but Jane had a lot, and I was sorry to see it go. However, the grinny maids seemed especially to admire my plump lips and warm, close-set seam.

During this initiatory period we were fitted for our clothes, and about these a word should be said. For it was bizarre in the extreme. The general uniform was of a sensible grey worsted, being a tunic that fitted closely to the waist, with open surplice neck and short sleeves. We wore no pinafores. Now I had gone short-skirted at Gateshead but this one-piece Grecian garment scarce covered at all, below. What passed for a skirt had better have been called a softly flaring bib. We four crimsoned when we realized this was all we were to wear, but for tautly tethered stockings, below the waist. There was a leathern belt.

The skirt, if such it might be called, was not allowed to do more than just cover the behind, and when we walked this derisory morsel of material did not even perform that office. Indeed, among the great girls, or Majors, it was something of a fashion when I was at Lowood even to further shorten the hems, so that the skirt lay on the shelf of the crupper exposing the plumply knickered undercurves. It was a sort of brazen pout of the buttock base, all the more tauntingly on display when there were some weals to show. But woe to any Minnie who shortened to this extent.

Lowood girls wore inky steeple heels, going over

on which was punishable. They made striding impossible. Short mincing steps were the most practical. Our stockings were coal-hued, drum-taut, and very high, being secured with satin garters of the knicker color I shall describe below, the school emblem on a clasp facing out at each thigh. The first garment we put on each morning was a short black corset of stiffly boned black leather. We fastened each other into these and the girl who laced was thrashed alongside the culprit whose corset was not tight enough. Any loosening of laces was of course frowned upon and would instantly result in a tingling sensation in the fatty portions of one's anatomy. There were times when I scarcely seemed able to breathe my first quarter at Lowood. I was a solid cylinder from rib-cage to rump, creaked when I walked, bent precariously, toppled when I curtseyed, and turned slowly, like a tube.

The busk in front was short but mercilessly stiff, and curved inwards, so that the rump was arched back. So stiff was one above that one became peculiarly conscious of this part of the body, as it rolled in motion, in what was called the typical Lowood walk. One was not intended, in Miss Temple's words, to throw oneself about like a prostitute. There were times those first days when I felt all rump.

Ten white bone buttons were affixed to the fore of those corsets, and ten to the back. To these were attached—oh cherished possessions (and daily changed)—one's knickers. These were of exquisitely fine cambric stuff of a silky feel and varied in color: Minnies wore the palest shade of rose, Minors of blue, Majors of clear transparent white, through which their buttocks bloomed. How envious one

soon became of these pale shades of glory, with their matching garters, to say nothing of the satin ribbon tightening their base. It was as if one passed through gradations of glory, from the pale human soul to brighten to the seraph! How the great girls flaunted theirs, tossing a leg up on a bench or leaning forward by a fire to show their seniority, and rank. To say these knickers were skin-tight would be an understatement. They were absolutely one's skin, and entirely but only covered the swelling cheeks. The sulcus was not shown, except at the side of the thigh of some especially fatted girl. The "leg" ribbons were taut and tailoring and tension were such that the cleft of the cheeks was completely followed. They made the buttocks stand out separately, in fact, firming and ripening their surfaces for the juicy cuts of the rod. These could indeed be clearly seen through the thinly textured covering.

Dress is important to a girl and anyone who knows a girl's growing mind can picture the dismay with which we four greeted the undergarment to be worn by new girls, until graduation into the Minimus class. Our knickers were of drab navy blue and made of common thin cotton. What is more they extended somewhat down the thigh, thus by their constant visibility making our lowly status a public spectacle. They had no ribbons.

We were hoisted into these one by one. Indeed, the term for our state from now on was "New-knicks." Mine would scarcely pass over my bursting buttocks, thin as they were. One girl got a new pair and was obliged to scour the back parts with a pumice stone in order to make the stuff sufficiently threadbare, to provide no protection for her person.

"There," said the grinning maid as she helped me to fasten the buttons of the corset through the holes, "all ready for a whipping. And you'll be needing a larger size after some of the canings you'll get here."

How to bend? How even to sit? We were told that splitting these drawers by a brusque or unruly motion might bring on a flogging, but that to have them split under one was almost a good mark. I never saw a pair so split up at Lowood nor elsewhere. We four soon caught the trick of slightly dampening them in the morning against such an eventuality, though learning that this made them cling even more and, in the opinion of one lovely authority, made the cane sting more.

I should lastly explain that Prefects or monitors wore a similar garb, only of a royal blue merino, very soft and sensuous, with knickers to match. Mistresses alone sometimes liked to wear no knickers in their private rooms.

Theoretically, material modified the cuts we received but I do not think our gossamer coverings did so. There were even times when I truly considered that birch or cane bit and stung into one worse when knickered. The flesh was held firm; the cuts ate in like fiends. Furthermore, unbuttoning had to be careful and considered. The command "Take down your knickers" at Lowood meant freeing twenty pearl buttons, with plenty of time for reflection, before peeling the fabric from the loins. Knickers could be examined at any time, and often were at night. Any soiling, before or behind, meant punishment, with perhaps a strap round one's mouth keeping the offending garment in it all night. Only spots of blood, after a birching, were an honor.

Finally, with trembling hearts as well as quivering skirts, we were presented to Miss Temple, the Head. Her office lay at the top of some curved stairs and was very opulent. We had been instructed to prostrate ourselves in her presence, as was the rule: this meant to kneel with hands held behind the back and lower the forehead to the very ground, bare board or carpet, until the permission to rise was given.

It was, at once; and though shivering with dread, we met the friendly eyes of a plump woman of some forty years, wearing pince-nez. I remember she also wore a watch and had fleshy shoulders, but we were supposed to stare ahead of us in her presence, at a level with our own eyes.

There was no sign of severity about Miss Temple that day; I recall only noticing, with the quick observation of the young, a rapier-like switch of some shiny black substance lying along her polished desktop. But she seemed a gentle person, almost shy, with a soft fluid smile. Someone kind, you would say. We were to learn what heart this hid later.

For the nonce she confined herself to addressing a few words of welcome to us and catechizing us on the institution. When it came to my turn she asked, "Who was Naomi Brocklehurst?"

"The lady who built this house, Ma'am, as the tablet outside records, and whose son now overlooks and directs everything here."

"Why?"

"Because he is treasurer and manager of the establishment, Ma'am."

She seemed pleased and then asked, "Are you happy, Jane Eyre?"

I said yes, for I was. We were shortly dismissed, after reciting the rules, and that evening there was a tumult of great girls arriving and being assigned here and there. Though each and all had to reck the rod, there was a natural ebullience of girlish spirits which warmly cheered me. My life at Lowood had begun.

Thwlupp!

SIIIIIIX!

"Yaaaaow!" I yelled.

White-hot coals. A slicing razor. What was it like? No brand could have been worse. The ivory cane struck in agonizingly and I bunched my buttocks in speechless reply. It was the most rare and cruel cane there was.

Dear God, but halfway through and no respite in sight.

A satisfied man's growl sounded from behind me—"Jane, I do declare I've drawn."

6

Life at the institution began early. Promptly at six a great bell was clanged in the corridors and on pain of punishment every girl had to be out of bed before it had ceased ringing. I was in a dormitory of eight girls in all, from all three ranks of the school; the new-knicks had been separated and my only colleague was the inky-haired and petite Joan Walker. We were in the charge of a monitor or Dorm Head called Marjorie Parker, a slender girl.

The previous night, as we were getting to bed, this great girl had looked with a frown at a list in her hand and said, "You Jane Eyre?"

"Yes, Parker," I said.

"Three first thing tomorrow." Then she crossed the aisle and said to Joan Walker, "Three first thing tomorrow. For a week."

Accordingly, as the girls all jumped out of bed, blithely divested themselves of their nightgowns, and ran into the adjacent wash-room, we presented ourselves to Parker, who was already dressed in her soft blue merino. But she merely pointed—"After your cold baths."

So we scampered through to the tiled wash-room, nude like the rest.

It was spacious and cold, the windows having been left open all night in order (I later learnt) to sheet the great central bath, several yards wide, with ice. Every girl had to plunge into this on rising and then rub her body dry with a coarse towel. There were then basins on stands for each girl. Naturally there was much squealing and laughing as the girls ducked their warm bodies in the icy water, which splashed up and doused the rush-lights.

Joan and Jane, dripping, then went back into the dorm for their three. We had not been granted the sight of the implement, but Parker appeared from her little curtained recess at the top of three short stairs holding a long lean cane.

"You first," she said, pointing to me. "Bend over there. No, so. Like this."

She showed me how she wanted me, bending till her own soft skirt slid up, revealing plump knickered chubbies. I had to bend in front of her steps, a little more than half over, holding the top one. She gave me three terrifically licky cuts, the last of which straightened me scarlet-faced. Whether it was the cold morning, the icy tub, or what, those under-cuts

stung furiously and I kneaded my bottoms after them as never I had after six from any of the Reed children. I began to develop a respect for Lowood willow.

The other girls, some still towelling, gathered, grinning. It was now the turn of Joan. She bent gracefully, her nervous little bottoms looking very tender. She got three strong slices very low and hopped and pranced in place, mewling with pain, when they were over. The monitor said "All right," rather boredly, and went into her den.

It was now the time for lacing. The girl who did mine said, "Hurts more wet, don't you think? You wait till you see Matron's switch. Stand still, silly." We made our beds, tidied our frocks, slid hands up skin-taut stockings and stood at the head of our beds like soldiers on parade. It was the moment for daily inspection. The monitor went to the door to await the Matron's visit.

Presently we heard the tap-tap from the next dormitory and, preceded by the Duty Prefect of the day, the Matron swung in, to be greeted by a curtsey from Parker and frozen stillness from ourselves. My vision was limited, mostly to the tears in Joan Walker's eyes opposite me, for we had to look firmly ahead unless addressed. But the diurnal cortege was spectacular and should be mentioned here.

The Duty Prefect of the day wore a costume which was the envy of all, a charming soft Grecian chlamys of purest white, just covering her bottom and no more. It was kirtled with a gold girdle and a large gold L was emblazoned on the left breast. The outlines of her knickers were tantalizingly visible

through the material as she moved and her stockings were of golden brown.

The Matron was clad in black leather, though her skirt was not as short as Neil's. She was a brawny personage of fifty-five with a sour expression on her lined face, from which hairs erupted. She had the muscles of a man and swung herself into the room aggressively on her black crutches, for, yes, Mrs. Harden had but one leg. This was booted thigh-high in black leather and the stump of its severed twin indented the material of her skirt as she made forward.

She passed me, I was thankful, without so much as a glance, though the monitor following put a hand under my skirt behind, and felt my back-thrust rump, presumably to see that all was tight and tidy there. The girl to my right had to open her mouth and had her teeth inspected with a black-gloved hand. Another showed her ears. Unlike some of the other mistresses, Matron Harden inspired dread fear; she was a woman made up of equal parts of whalebone and iron, a brutal, low person under her impassive exterior. Wherever she went a long supple switch accompanied her right leg; its trainer or tail was braided and hard.

Finally, she had found a fault. I discerned some reproof on the other side of the dormitory. I did not look—at first—but a Minor, albeit a big girl of nearly seventeen, had been faulted for some matter connected with her bed; probably she had not made up one corner in the special way we were required to. I had to look. I looked.

With a wretched expression the girl stood back

from her bed, turned and bent over, grasping the rail at the bottom of it. The Duty monitor lifted up her tiny skirt, revealing firmly thrusting buttocks in their smokeblue veil of skintight knickers. There was a band of flesh below these, then the stockings. The Matron handed her right crutch to Parker and leaning on the other, stood well back.

She cut with astonishing venom. Once, twice, thrice, that switch bit wickedly into the young flesh. The dark weals showed as if written by some pencil. Her buttocks clenched, she clung perilously to the rail, her head back. She was panting.

"Bend right over, Crawford," said the Duty Prefect.

Ffffressp! Four.

The girl arched erect, clasping her bottoms and hissing with pain. I looked away. But some altercation ensued. It was evident the Matron was displeased with the culprit's performance; the girl had not waited for her permissive word to rise. She had been awarded a Demerit for recalcitrance under correction and would accordingly find herself getting four in the Duty Room that evening, the initiatory number for her class.

I believe we all gave a sigh of relief when that martinet in black leather left the room. Mine was echoed by Parker's hot whisper in my ear, "I ought to report you for turning and looking, Eyre. I am responsible for the discipline of this dorm to the Head. Now touch your toes twenty times." When I had done so and was flushing she said, "You will write me out a hundred times by tonight, 'I must stare straight ahead during Inspection.' Understand?"

"Yes, Parker."

The bell rang for breakfast. We trooped down in order of dormitories.

Great Hall was ruddy with gigantic log fires and the warmth of young bodies. The mistresses ate at a raised or "high" table at one end, the whole assembly awaiting the entry of the majestic Miss Temple, in a sweeping gown, who read Collect from a lectern and then Grace, before we might sit down to our gruel.

I was about to do so when I saw the girl who had been whipped in the dormitory remaining standing, and did so myself, recollecting just in time the school rule that any girl who had received cuts that day took her meals upright. There were already one or two to do so. I thanked my lucky stars I had remembered.

After copious commons there was a free period for our natural needs and preparation for classes. The relief of the inner person at Lowood institution was something I found particularly vexing, all my first year there. How trying it was day after day to be reduced to the rank of absolute mere children. For while the great girls had some privacy, the Minimus class and ourselves had to perform this function publicly in the presence of the Matron, in an upstairs room of the house.

Matron sat at a table, with a book, and we lined up beside it. She called out three names and three girls advanced to a small raised area before us. There in front of all they had to un-knicker and squat down over large shallow white pans, into which they had to "do their duty," as the saying went. We were given three or four minutes for this task of voiding our entrails, facing a wall, after which we were declared costive; the strains and grunts that ensued might

have seemed comical, were they not in such deadly earnest. For Matron was a merciless clysterer.

Once done, the girl then cleaned herself, re-knickered and showed her bowl to the Matron, who marked it down in her text. The girl then flushed it out at one side and gave it to the next, and so on.

The diet at Lowood was such—our porridge was replete with psyllium seeds—that stool was generally large, full, and unyielding. I have seen quite small girls, indeed, thump down great massy turds, steaming in the basin, worthy of some stable. But this first day the aperient had not had its effect and of the thirteen of our number, for the Minnie class was nine, with us four to add, three were declared costive. Of these poor Joan Walker's efforts to relieve herself had been quite pathetic. I saw these girls morosely eyeing the saucepan of oil heating over the flame, their knickers round their ankles, as I quit the chamber.

The clyster was an old-fashioned one, with a long beak with a crook in it. The injection was of hot olive oil, usually given with a single drive of the plunger. Administered quite bent over, it seemed to shoot up its thick hot jet right into us, and one was soon trampling the boards uncomfortably after it. The enema had to be held for several minutes, on pain of cuts. Final relief was luxurious. Repetition of the offense was in fact rewarded with your class score of cuts (thankfully only three for mine) after the clystering. A further costivity would rate cuts both before and after. No one to my knowledge ever had them during; they were that merciful at Lowood, at least.

At classes, which began shortly after, one stocked

one's own ankles at small desks and sat one's knickered seat on hard deal wood. Fidgeting was especially frowned on. My first class was in Latin, with Miss Oakes, a young cheerful blonde woman. It was uneventful. I knew my Latin. The second was likewise, in French with pretty dark-eyed Madame Pierrot.

Towards the end of this lesson, after a *dictée,* a big girl was found guilty of some fault. She had to stand up and bend forward right down over her desk. Her corset made a hard rap as she did so. Her skirt hardly had to be raised, but was so. The basin of her buttocks was spread in the pellucid knickers—white, for she was a Major girl, all the pedagogic classes being intermixed. Madame Pierrot gave her then five whistling, wristy slices with her cane; these cuts were administered vertically, straight-down, there being scarce room for a swing back. They bit crisply into the upper curves and seemed to cause the culprit some discomfort; though she made not a sound, the fatty cheeks cringed and clenched in expressively. She was made to stand for the rest of the period, with her skirt in a roll at her waist. She watched the weals darkening in hue, for she was in a forward row.

After this came a break period, during which we were allowed milk and biscuits, and were addressed in a friendly fashion by Miss Temple. I began to think my fears had been excessive. But my next hour was to be in Greek, with Miss Scatcherd, and I knew I had to be on my toes.

Like the Matron, this mistress was universally dreaded; she had been known to start off a term by flogging an entire form. She was a short dark un-

smiling woman with high cheekbones and big rather slanting eyes, under silky black hair. She longed to cut into and cane us and did so pitilessly. I had been warned to stay out of her path and meant to do so. She had a way of making a girl feel throughly flogged, a talent she shared with Mr. Brocklehurst, forsooth.

There was the silence as of death as she came into the room, holding a cold yellow cane of great length. This she flexed and bent as she paraded silently up and down our aisle, inspectingly. My shoulders rippled as she passed. Lastly, she stood on her dais confronting us, legs astride, her head back and her glossy eyes shining. She was the living picture of one who longed to use the rod, and it was not long before she did.

"The trouble with you girls is, you're spoilt," she pronounced finally. "You're all lazy and idle and spoilt. You need more whipping. Well, this term I'm going to see that you get it. There's going to be an order of the birch for the first girl I find insolent." Our mild faces and lowly mien hardly betokened much mutiny, but the harangue continued: "I mean to make a lesson, of one of you, to start this term off on the right foot. Well, any volunteers? Come," she said with ironic smile, "I won't kill you." Then her eyes hardened and she snapped, "Helen Burns. Stand out."

A big dark girl stood up. I had remarked her already, for her soft, luminous beauty and gentleness of expression. Though nigh on eighteen, this girl had been kept back in the Minor class by Miss Scatcherd's enmity. Tall and serene, Helen Burns had exceptionally long legs with full round calves,

soft knees, and widely tapering thigs. Under their morsel of material her hips had a slumbrous roll, full of flesh. I sat up straight. This great girl was going to be punished. In the eye of a neighbor I caught the same eager gleam that I had seen in Eliza's during the caning of her sister. Helen Burns stood before the mistress, dwarfing her by a head.

"Turn and face the class," came the command; and then, "Take down your knickers."

When this had been accomplished, and the garment lay in miserable blue wrinkles round her ankles, she was bidden roll her skirtlet up into her belt. Interest went from extreme to acute. My fingers quivered at the spectacle with a sentiment of unavailing and impotent anger. The girl was going to be whipped for—nothing! And not a feature of her pensive face altered its ordinary expression. The haired slot of her thickly seamed sex stared at us from the sill at the top of her close-joined thighs. She was most richly bushed, the transverse bar of the T her hair formed there extending widely across her belly and being crimped into close curls by the knicker pressure.

"Dawes!" came the command. "Backboard."

A little girl went to get one from the stack at the side. The Lowood version of this celebrated instrument was characteristically unpleasant, the board to which we were yoked being a thick and heavy plank. The neck strap was affixed, then the two thongs diagonally round the body under the armpits. Then she held out her arms and had her wrists strapped behind the board at either end projecting from her shoulders. After my first hour in one of these I felt

as if my arms were leaving their sockets, and its application was entirely excessive now.

"Lean forward, Burns. Enough."

Miss Scatcherd stood back, measured aim, and with a tigerish pace that sent her own pleats swinging thrashed into the proferred buttocks. These visibly moved under the whirry *whuck* of impact, but Burns' face did not alter. Nor did she flinch at the second or third. After a long silence the fourth, and final for her class, was given.

The mistress looked into the girl's face.

"Hardened thing! You will have another cut, since you are of age for a Major."

At this injustice the trace of a tear glistened on Burns' round cheek. The cut was a vicious one and made her gasp.

"Turn round and lean forward," said Miss Scatcherd. "Show your marks."

It was hard for the girl to obey, harnessed heavily as she was, and she had to bend her knees to support herself doing so. The cane had clawed its dark lines close at her underseat. The anal crater was plumply sunk. Finally she was made to stand on a high stool with her marked back to the class; she climbed up the rungs and perched there perilously, in view of all, her welts empurpling.

"Anyone else for a licking?" Miss Scatcherd asked, her eyes snapping. "I mean to flog you all this term."

Only when she had put her ominous instrument aside did I breathe again. The lesson followed without further incident but for one girl, a fidgeter, I fear, being sent from the room to have a saddle strap

put on her. This horrid device was a strip affixed to the busk of the corset in front, drawn through the sex lips and up the anal valley behind to be buckled tightly there. The most moderate version was a rather hard round strap, like the collar of a dog and it cut you in two when you walked. Bending was appalling. The girl re-entered in mincing gait, frowning, and Miss Scatcherd inspected the strap's tension. While the girl winced with pain she tried to draw it up one notch, but could not. The poor creature sat down at her desk extremely gingerly. As we filed out Miss Scatcherd called me to her and inspected my knickers, running her hand in front over my hairless bulge for any wetness. Fortunately all was dry and so I scaped off.

The day passed uneventfully enough. In a break period in the afternoon I wandered among the forms and tables and laughing groups to seek out Helen Burns. She was alone, reading, an absorbed, silent, abstracted figure in a chair by a fireplace. I asked her about the book, and it was *Rasselas*. Her great beauty again struck me.

"That teacher, Miss Scatcherd, was cruel to you," I said. But she only shook her head.

"Not particularly. She can hit far harder than that."

"But you hadn't done anything!" I objected.

"Still, it did me good. I will remember, and be more careful in future."

"If I were in your place I should hate her. It seems disgraceful to be flogged so, a great girl like you, bared and before us all."

Helen Burns looked at me steadily. At last she

said, "Scatcherd and Mrs. Harden are the only ones who beat us with dislike. The rest do so in love. I deserve to be whipped and I fret if I am not, at least once a week. You see this." She drew my attention to a large white button pinned on her tunic at the left shoulder. I read the word IDLE upon it. "Miss Smith gave me this Demerit. I forgot a rule. This means that tonight I shall get four benders, in the Duty Room. You know what they are, don't you?" I nodded. I did. "Yes, four tremendous whistlers over the board, with the Duty cane. You've seen those, haven't you?"

"Yes."

" 'Twill hurt twice as much as those flicks this morning. Four juicy beauties just above the fold, enough to make you jump out of your skin. But that girl over there"—she indicated a plump back—"she must have eight this evening. Two Demerits. She'll howl before it's over with a bit of luck. Yes, fortunately she is senior to me and I shall watch it before getting mine. It always increases the tension for me."

I heard her with wonder. I could not comprehend this doctrine of endurance; and still less could I understand the forbearance she expressed for her chastiser.

"Are you so in love with punishment then?" I asked her.

"I need it, I get it," was the simple answer. Then she went on, "One day before I leave Lowood I should like to see if I could go a full count with the soko, in front of the school. Oh! you've no idea how our birches sting. After you've gone a dozen

your whole being feels beat. And Neil has ways of making you so tender behind, before you go up. There's the mustard poultice for one. Heavens, how those first cuts sting. And then you realize you have to go to thirty, or even more, with the last ones drawn out longer and longer till you're yelping like a puppy."

I wondered away, puzzled but excited. I knew that punctually at nine the Duty Prefect of the day would enter evening preparation and collect the quaking culprits on Demerits for their quotas of corrective agony. They would be bared and bent over the celebrated board and their backsides lashed with that remedial rod. Each would take to bed with her the witness of weals well written on her flesh, and a glowing pain to be assuaged by the probing finger. . . .

I wrote on, as darkness came and the rush-lights were lit in the rooms.

At ten minutes before six o'clock I went to present my lines to Marjorie Parker, the monitor who was my Dorm Head. I had laboured long over these, while the others had been able to stroll in the gardens, and I was proud of what I had done. The writing was meticulous.

Each monitor at Lowood had a small private room, as her personal study. I knocked and went in Parker's. It was modestly but cheerfully furnished, with a fire blazing in the grate. The girl was working at a desk.

"Oh it's you, Eyre," she said.

"I've brought you my lines."

I approached her but she did not deign to look up

for quite some minutes. When she as last did so it was with a hostile expression on her rather ordinary face. She stood up and, saying "These are no good," took the lines from me; looking me deliberately in the eye, she tore them and tossed them on the flames. A stab of anger flashed through my heart, and when she reached for a small yellow square of paper hot tears of injustice pressed behind my eyes.

At the same time my lips quivered, my stomach went hollow. I was going to get my first "Yellow."

No prefect was allowed to chastise personally at Lowood without permission. The dormitory cuts we new-knicks were receiving were on superior order. In all other cases the monitor had to fill in a form which the offender had to take to a mistress for signature. She could only give the number appurtaining to the girl's class and furthermore—only over knickers. The cuts had all to be on the buttocks, too. Never in my time at the school did I know a senior girl abuse these privileges. The most merciless punishment would have been the result. There had been some monitor who had given more than the proper number, it seemed, in the days before I came. The girl she had whipped showed her bottom to a mistress and the older one was had up at Assembly, reduced to the rank of Minimus, her head wholly shaved and then her bottom brutally beaten by Mr. Brocklehurst. Thereafter until the end of that term she received a severe birching every Friday, in front of all the school.

The Yellow was a very simple request for punishment. Mine, when I took it from Parker, looked like this:

Jane Eyre
PERMISSION TO GIVE . . . .
3
STROKES . . . .
Marjorie Parker
ORDER OF . . . .
COUNTERSIGNED . . . .

"Get a good cane," said the girl.

Anger emboldened me. "You did not look at them. The lines were well done."

She glared at me coldly. "You have the right to appeal, new-knick. But I must say it's not much gone in for here. My word will count against yours, and a failed appeal always means double the cuts, by the Duty Mistress with a Duty cane."

"I shall not appeal," I said as evenly as I might. "But I do not deserve flogging."

"You're going to get it," said she. "And if you're not careful, Eyre, you'll get another Yellow for lip."

Tears were pricking at my eyes as I sought out a mistress, in the Common Room. The woman looked up from her book, signed mechanically, said "I hope it hurts," and went on with her reading. I went down again and tried to find a rod that would hurt less in a classroom. But they were all beastly whippy things. I stood outside the door with it in my hands. My heart was in my boots but a fury of injustice beat up in my breast. I would not show this great girl my smart, however it might be.

There was another girl with her this time, whose name I did not know. She grinned at me and said to her friend, "Oh lovely and chubby!"

Parker took the chit and cane and made me stand

in front of the fireplace, leaning forward slightly and gripping the mantlepiece. The skirt was raised from my rounded bottom and put in my belt all round.

"Oh, lovely bum"

Three, I thought, only three.

She took an absurdly long time positioning me. "Brace back your knees more. Press back. Stick out your bum. Arch your back more, so that it spreads. Tighten your knickers." I made no movement at this since how might they be any tighter?

Indeed, the other girl laughed and said, "They're bursting."

The first cut whistled into me. Such was my indignation, such courage did my anger give me, that I veritably believe I made no move beyond the indentation of my flesh behind. My jaws were locked as one.

"Lower," said the girl watching, in a soft tone.

"No I'll put them all across the center. She's so fat down there."

There was a long pause. The heat was flaming up. Heavens, how it stung! Far more than that morning. The second whipped in like lightning. My head rang, as if my ears had been boxed. Infernal! My breath harshened, the inside of my rump cheeks wriggled together, but otherwise I made no sign.

"I tell you, Marj, you're not hurting her enough."

"She's so fat, and beside this cane is too light."

"Bend her double and give her this last one low."

"Oh, all right. Eyre, bend right over and touch your toes. Come on, right down, as hard as you can."

"There," said her mentor. "Now cut under her."

The pain was mounting miserably. It was a really stingy cane, a brute. After a long wait again the girl

gave the third. I gasped, but that was all. I managed to keep down until with a bored "All right," my tormentress tossed her cane to one side. Though my hands longed to grasp my seat I controlled myself to make them collect the wicked instrument and, face blazing but otherwise composed, I said to Parker, "Is there anything else you want?"

"Three more like that tonight, mind."

I picked up the cane and walked steadily towards the door. I did not want them to see the tears that were threatening to burst behind my eyes. It was ridiculous that three could sting up so, and I think it was my sense of injustice that made them do so.

I negotiated a bend in the the corridor but got no further. An access of white-hot flame scalded me unspeakably, for the true pain of a caning is only felt some seconds after it is over. I dropped the horrid implement and grabbed my buttocks, hoping that by rubbing them I could ease some of the awful smart. There was a step but I did not notice.

"I say. Someone not a million miles away with a well-whipped bottom. Does it hurt a lot?"

I looked up. Pretty Miss Miller's blue eyes danced into mine. "Terribly, Miss," I said, sniffling. I pushed the back of one hand into my right eye.

"What did you get?"

"Three, Miss. From Parker."

"Is that all?" She laughed merrily, then said, "And don't you usually curtsey when a mistress comes by?"

"S-sorry, Miss." I ducked a knee hastily.

"I'll let you off this time, don't look so crestfallen; though next it'll be three real whistlers in the Duty Room. I tell you what, as it's really your first

day I'll give you a treat. Run and put that cane away and come back here."

I hastened to do as bid. I liked plump, dark Miss Miller, always brimming with cheerful laughter. Once again I felt I had a friend.

When I rejoined her she motioned me forward, saying "Quick, quick." And when I fell into step behind her as we were supposed, she warmly took my arm and brought me beside her. Thus we went up the long carpeted main stair.

"Feeling better now, Jane Eyre?"

"Much, thank you, Miss," I answered, with grateful smile.

"All the same, I wonder at three making you blub."

"These canes . . . are so terribly stingy and, and licky, Miss."

She chuckled. "All the more reason to keep your sensitive skin out of the light, Jane. Were they low?" Her hand was feeling behind me, cupping under my skirt. I winced expressively.

"The last one was."

She laughed again. "By the time you leave here you'll be taking ten like that as a matter of course. Or almost. Just you wait and see."

We were now navigating deserted upstairs passages, making for the wing where the mistresses had their chambers. The woman was flushed and hot, almost holding me to her as we went. I was curious as to what "treat" she was taking me, like any child, and answer soon came. She half-whispered in one ear:

"I am going to whip a good big Minor girl with the birch. Come, won't that cheer you up, Jane? To

see the twigs singing into someone else's skin? Oh there's nothing like it. Our birches sting like fury, you ought to know by now, having put some up. I cannot tell you, my child, how completely alive I feel at this moment. Ah, here we are."

Miss Miller all but licked her lips. A well-grown girl with round, though not heavy, hips was standing like a sentry in front of the mistress' door. She was quite pale of face, though expressionless. Already I observed myself, in Lowood habit, assessing the nether hemispheres.

The mistress strode in before us.

"Come in, Eleanor," she said. "I'm going to birch your buttocks. Clear the room with Jane Eyre and let me get at you, then."

While I helped the poor girl, obviously in palpitating apprehension, push back chairs and a table to clear a large space in the center of the comfortable room, the mistress proceeded briskly to an earthenware pot from which she drew out a dripping verge. The lithe instrument was soon hissing through the air.

I had, in my under-week of preparation, indeed confectioned a number of these fearful rods. Miss Miller evidently favored the spare variety, hers having only three or four withes. But all were literal whips, lean whippy limbs toughened by pickling in vinegar, then the standing brine, toughly budded, and latticed with thin wire up their length. The girl gulped with dismay at these monitory preparatives. She was clearly very frightened. The rod looked as long as her.

"Tell Jane Eyre what you're here for."

The girl looked at me and said in an impassive

painstaking way: "To be whipped by the birch-rod for Inattention."

"Where?"

As if correcting herself the girl stammered, "To be whipped across the buttocks by the birch-rod, Miss. For Inattention."

"First this term?"

"Y-yes, Miss."

Again that tell-tale gulp. This was no Helen Burns. A heat was warming up in me at the spectacle, I had to confess.

"Well let's make it a good one. I feel in just the right mood. Do up your skirt." As the girl, with a lost look, rolled it up into her belt, the mistress snapped. "Retain your knickers. I like the sound. Besides, I still have the ambition to split a pair." Her eyes shone. She grinned maliciously and a bubble of saliva shone on her ivory teeth. "Turn round now, Eleanor. Yes a fine impudent pair. Let's see if we can thrash a little attention into them. Stand straight, do not bend. Hands clasped before you, so. Nice and relaxed. Any clenching and it's cut over. Let's see you show a new-knick how to bear it. Don't they stand out well for it, Jane Eyre?"

I freely admitted that they did. Sheened in the transparent pale blue stuff, in which not a wrinkle might be seen and against which the darker blue of the leg ribbons stood in pretty contrast, it was a proud pair, indeed. The cheeks were round, sturdy and well protruding, with deep division (into which the gauzy material fitted) and not so much overhang as mine. The jut from the corset back was pronounced.

"Oh Good Heavens, I can't wait to get at them."

The mistress gave her creámy gurgle of mirth and, turning, slipped fingers under her own under-garment and quickly slid it down over her stockings and off. She winked at me in complicity. "I always whip better knickerless." She turned for her rod and the swing of skirt gave me a glimpse of her own opulent hams. My caning was now a pleasant gluteal warmth that spread through my being, and I was beginning to feel my heart pounding up in a new way. I remembered Eliza's look during the thrashing of her sister by Mr. Brocklehurst. Our Lowood rods were always bound at the holding end by twine, but Miss Miller took a wet rag and wound it around hers. The twigs quivered livingly under the expectant seat as she took aim and I realized that her own body was a-tremble, too.

"You may count the cuts, Jane. You will stand in front of her and count aloud. What is more she will smile—do you hear, Eleanor?—and you will tell me if she does not retain that smile throughout. 'Twill be excellent control of her lower emotions. Good Lord, the birch is pure poetry, is it not!"

I went to my place before the wretched victim. She had put on a rigid absurd smile and clasped her hands at her lap.

Miss Miller stepped back. "Here it comes," she said in a low voice, as if talking to herself. "Twelve beauties right across your you-know-where."

She paced and cut. The twigs seemed veritably to double before they lashed, ending in their dry whip as they met firm flesh. The sound made me jump and I quickly got out "One, Miss" in a startled tone.

A pause and another long sweep—"Two."

The girl gasped but retained her rigidity of grin. The third lapped round her wickedly.

"Three!"

"Plenty more to go, eh, Jane Eyre!"

It was truly a whipping. The birch thrashed the whole seat and I got a sense of its clawing sting as Eleanor bowed or jerked her upper body, then ducked her legs with hisses of pain.

"Brace back your knees."

We had got to seven. The poor girl's face was a mockery of mirth; her grin had become a grimace, her forehead a single frown. Eight . . . nine . . . she shot her hands back, then recovered.

"I ought to give you an extra for that!"

Zzzzsch!

"Ten!"

"Ow!" The girl ducked, fisting her fingers in her groin. "Oh please, Miss," she whispered in a broken tone.

"What is it now?" asked Miss Miller; she was smiling broadly herself.

The girl was silent for a few seconds, then got out a single, sobbed word—"Mercy!"

"What do you mean, mercy, Eleanor?"

"Please let me off the last two, Miss."

"They're going to do you the most good of all."

"I . . . I can't take them . . . unless you tie me, please."

"Nonsense. Stand up straight and show a little courage. And get that smile back on your face, quick. As a matter of fact I shall give you three for making such a fuss. Yes, we'll make it a butcher's dozen as Mr. Brocklehurst invariably gives, and no rubbing after. You've hardly felt a thing. I haven't even drawn yet."

Slowly the girl straightened herself. Squeezing shut

her eyes she forced the grin on her face again, which was quite completely contorted. Remorselessly the twigs bit in, one, twice, thrice. At the last, a ferocious cut, the girl gave a long moaning "Oooooh!" She sank to her knees with a thud and bowed over, rocking in speechless pain, crossing her arms to keep her rebellious hands from rubbing.

"Jane, quick," I heard in an almost mischievous hiss. "A birched buttock. Look."

I looked. The streaks stood out sharply on the now bent cheeks, on the right of which they were darkly purpling and had lapped round the hip. I thought I saw a speck of blood on the stuff, but was not sure.

"I cut long," said Miss Miller reflectively. Then to the girl, "You birch well, Eleanor. Feeling sorry for yourself? Well, get that bottom out of here unless you want some more on those."

The girl curtseyed and obeyed, her face writhen. When I looked back Miss Miller was standing with feet widely apart and the hem of her skirt lifted in front; I saw a strong black curly bush and a wetly gleaming seam. Her face was scarlet, her breathing harsh.

"Jane Eyre! do you know how to?"

"Yes, Miss," I said meekly, and truthfully. Eliza's training was not to go for nothing here, then. I knelt on the carpet, among the shards of twig.

"Quick! My clit's like an iron spring. Oh my God yes . . . get your tongue . . . and, and lick, suck . . . suck it like that, squeeze it in your lips . . . oh my God wasn't it heaven when she begged for mercy . . . Jane, Jane, good Heavens you know how to . . . and grab my bottoms behind, yes, yes yeeeeees. . . ."

When I was finally allowed to get up and wipe my mouth, Miss Miller smiled as she collapsed into a chair with a sigh. She straddled one leg over an arm and I could see the slick sweat on her haired sex.

"Where did you learn to be so expert, Jane Eyre? Good Lord, I can't think when I ever let a new-knick do that to me." She gave her gurgle of mirth. "You realize you've just enjoyed a great favor and you realize, too, that this will only make me the more eager to whip you. Will you writhe nicely, do you think?"

"I expect so, Miss."

"Know what the scum buss is?"

"Yes, Miss."

"What?"

"Tongue up the anus, Miss."

"Tongue *right* up the anus, you monkey," she chuckled. "And kept there till you taste a bit of shit. Now run along with you. I promised you a treat and I gave you one, I think."

That night Helen Burns was collected from prep with four other culprits. She went to her doom impassively. The girl to get eight was crying softly as she left. We later learnt—for Dorm talk was full of these "swishings"—that she got a magisterial flogging on the underhams, and that the last two had made her yell. Parker's injustice still rankled and I took my three from her before the dorm stoically, though it was hard to keep my hands outside the bedsheets, as required, for Matron's inspection, later. As the lights were doused I realized that my first day at Lowood had passed, that I had had nine, and that the first thing I would be conscious of upon awakening was corporeal pain.

Phhhhhhrrrrp!

The seventh hewed mercilessly into me, driving my poor bum upwards. Merciful Heaven, what agony! I twisted and shook in the triangle. The punishment was attaining a new plane and a more ferocious rigor. A fierce fart escaped me.

I dashed my head back. My whole buttock felt on fire though he had but only slightly broadened the band of blue weal. I clenched in, then cambered back involuntarily—and Mr. Rochester chose his moment and cut in again!

7

My initiatory week at Lowood proceeded without anything untoward. Until that fateful Thursday. Come Monday and we would be enrolled in the Minimus class, and regular tasks and occupations be assigned us. No more would we be lowly new-knicks. How eagerly we four looked forward to that small elevation in our humble stations.

Repetitions in history, grammar, geography, writing, arithmetic were all measured by the block. Miss Smith put into my hands a border of muslin one afternoon. A class was standing around the chair of Miss Scatcherd who was reading. It was English history and, sure enough, I soon heard the inevitable exhortations—"Burns, you are standing on the side

of your shoe, turn your toes out immediately," "Burns, you poke your chin most unpleasantly, draw it in," "Burns, I will not have you before me in that attitude."

A slim cane was soon called for and this time the mistress gave the favor of its administration to another great girl who plied it across Helen's bottom with positive relish.

It must not be thought, however, that our days were drear. Far from it. It is true there were always those whippy little licks in the dorm of a morning, but I managed to keep my hide reasonably inconspicuous and intact for the first half of that week. Moreover, girlish ebullience is impossible to repress and, well fed, kept warm, our spirits were generally high. There was love at Lowood, as never there had been under Mrs. Reed's stern roof. We also had a strong *esprit de corps.*

The day after I had seen the girl called Eleanor "swished" by Miss Miller I met her in a corridor. Imagining that she might not want to meet the witness of her discomfiture, if not disgrace, I was about to hasten on when the other detained me. She was smiling widely at me, obviously without a care in the world.

"You're Eyre, aren't you?"

"Yes, Scott-James."

"Sorry I didn't do better in that birching."

"I thought you . . . took it very well," I consoled, dubiously.

She shook her head decisively. "Rotten show. It was lack of practice. I don't get it in the hols, you see. And that tenth was a whistler."

"What did she mean by cutting . . . long?"

"It means that the twigs lap round your side, silly. Look."

She turned and bent forward, lifting what was left of her skirt; the traceries of stripes were still visible through the transparent veil of blue. She chuckled as she straightened. "Blue, brown, green, yellow, all the colors of the rainbow, eh? Miller can always be relied on to be tight. I worship her, really."

With that she strode on, insouciantly.

That evening I had the pleasure of seeing my colleague Susan Cuningham, who I was liking less and less, get a nice "tight" caning and the following morning a great girl was chastised publicly, before the whole school, in Assembly, which was very salutory. But on Thursday my world fell about me.

Throughout the morning the lessons had seemed long and hard and I was fortunate to get through them without cuts. I was looking forward to the play-hour when we came in from exercise that afternoon. The grounds of Lowood were a large enclosure, surrounded with walls so high as to exclude every glimpse of prospect. It was an inclement day for out-of-door exercise, soaking wet underfoot and with a drizzling yellow fog. Yet we were herded for a dismal run around the extent, conducted by the gym mistress Miss Boyden. At last, wet through and panting like puppies, we returned to the communal changing-room, a large boarded room with a tiled bath steaming with hot water set at one end. Two undermistresses, Seale and Hall, were "taking" this changing-room and I saw them laughing and chatting at one side as I ran in; Miss Seale was holding the inevitable cane.

Now it was a traditional that the last girl in from

exercise got cuts. And I duly saw a Minor bend down for four sweeping stripes across her solid seat, over which the wet knickers were taut as skins. Then I was undressing fast for the bath. There was also a custom that the last girl out of the room also got a dose.

"Let's see, Maud, let's see," the girls chorussed as the Minor who had been punished advanced naked, her face creased and holding her chubbies, to the splashing throng of pink bodies. She duly showed her back for us.

"She didn't have to hit that hard," said the girl sulkily as she eased her offended parts into the soapy, steaming water. Georgy Reed's similar opinion came to mind.

Unluckily the mistress had approached. Rapping her cane on the side of our bath she said, "When I want criticism of my activities, Maud, I'll ask for it."

"Sorry, Miss," the girl gulped hastily.

"Rather late, I fear. You'll take two Demerits for Impertinence."

There was a shocked hush at this. Two Demerits for a Minor meant facing up to eight with a Duty cane that night. The girl said "Thank you, Miss," impassively, and reached for a sponge.

The hubbub round the tub did not resume. Soon the room was in silence while girls dried themselves, folded clothes tidily in lockers, and strove to get dressed. Oh, all those knicker buttons!

I was aware of girls leaving and did not become conscious of my own tardiness until there were but a handful of junior girls left, all straightening stockings and drying necks.

Miss Hall it was now who was smilingly swinging the cane. "Come on, Illingsworth. Buck up, Mary. Hurry, Eyre. I'm dying to get at one of you."

She was a tall blonde woman in her twenties. A girl scampered out. There were two of us left. Those buttons . . . I should have to leave one undone, for Illingsworth was at the door. With a gasp I made for it, trying to thrust in front of her. For a second we were wedged there, then, with a laugh, Miss Seale pulled me strongly back by an earlobe.

"Oh no, you don't. Come on you!"

"Please," I quavered, quaking. "I tried."

"Well, you'll just have to try again harder, won't you."

They were both grinning and laughing at me. These few cuts seemed to be matters of amusement to them, but we knew how viciously they stung.

"What are you waiting for? Bend over, Jane Eyre!"

I put my hands on my knees. "Sealey," as we called her, a plump, dark junior mistress, flipped up my skirt behind. "Hullo, hullo. Button undone. Can't have this, can we!" She did it up and stroked the bursting globes.

I set myself for it. Parker had by now written twenty-one dorm lines, and three in her study, across my lower person. One place, on the right, was extremely tender and contused.

Miss Hall took a long time. And a long run. About three springy paces of her endless legs—and then it came, wrapping itself fiendishly about me.

THWWLLICK! Full across.

"Haow!"

Whether it was that my flesh was warm and wettish, from run and tub, the swipe streaked atrocious pain up me. I waited, panting.

THWLLLCKK!

"Yow!"

A long, long pause and then the scalding third. I leapt up and hopped and danced in front of their grinning faces. Still puffing I ducked a curtsey and was about to escape when again I was lugged back once more by the earlobe. It was a humiliating process.

"You don't think we're letting you off for undone buttons, do you?"

"Oh Miss, please, have a heart."

"Bend over."

Three more frightful slices. I was growing very sore. Finally, for being "all wet behind one ear," I was adjudicated three more still. Sealey gave me these, and I had to bend and put my hands on the floor and part my legs widely behind me. They were excruciating and I hobbled from the room, mewling.

An hour later the Duty monitor for the day, a great girl called Hutchinson, swirled past me in a side corridor, looking sumptuous in her white.

"Oh I say, Eyre." She turned back and felt into a little leathern bag at her waist. "I nearly forgot. You're on Demerit tonight. Untidy locker on inspection."

She handed me a button with UNTIDY on it. My lips were giving way. Tears mutinied to my eyes.

"Ber but I've just had nine. . . ."

"Well, you'll get three more, won't you. Oakes is on Duty and she always makes it hurt. Cheer up!" And she patted my cheek. "It won't kill you, quite."

I was "up" for my first Duty caning. My stomach

shrank, my sides caved in. Sure enough, the dreaded list went up shortly before Evening Hall.

"Hard cheese, Eyre," said a voice in the crowd around it.

"Good Lord, Maud is in for eight!"

There were six names: I was to suffer last.

"Jennifer's hardly going to have much fun."

The notice, whose letters squirmed like snakes before my eyes, read:

The following will attend on the Duty Mistress at 9.00 p.m.

Drayne, J	Tardy	5	
Palmer, T.	Idle	4	
Morris, M.	Pert	4	
	"	4	[this was Maud]
Wragg, T.	Inattentive	3	
Ponsonby, E.	Idle	3	
Eyre, J.	Untidy	3	

Needless to describe the content of the hours that passed between that simple reading and our evening prep where, eyes glazing over well-bethumbed Ovid or stealing a crucial glance at the clock above, the six culprits sat with cringing skins and sinking stomachs, occasionally receiving the sly glances of other girls.

Promptly on the chime of nine Hutchinson strode in and went up to the mistress in supervision. Then she came down the aisles collecting us. She tapped me on the shoulder with a whispered "Wanted," and I hectically amassed my books in my desk and followed the rest out. Without the door she called our roll to see that all were present, then said "Hurry up, get into line. Now follow me." We did so to the far

end of the building where we went down some wide steps to the formal Duty chamber. It was the most miserable rank imaginable who lined up along the wall one side of this, while the Prefect stood opposite with the great black Demerit book in one hand. After some minutes a few senior girls appeared, and chatted with Hutchinson; they liked to see the punished girls come out after their chastisement and squirm and writhe their way up the stairs. Finally, the sharp staccato of a mistress's high heels might be heard. Miss Oakes came into view.

The Latin mistress was young and energetic, with short curly blonde hair and square shoulders on a chunky body. Her close-fitting black velvet tunic, with the big L in gold on the left breast, hung without a fold from the bursting body, while the skirt hem barely covered the buttocks, under which smoky stockings were tautly gartered. She bounced into the room as we curtseyed and Hutchinson followed in with her.

One of the great girls at the side said, "Ouch . . . ouch . . . whew!"

I took a deep breath. Apprehension was filling me wholly. We were going to get it. There was no avoidance now. The ineluctability, the march of events, had us in its sway and I fear that just in front of me Thomasina ("Tommy") Wragg was gently crying.

Then the door abruptly opened and the monitor called, "Come in."

We entered and lined up, one behind the other, on one side of the room. This was timbered and raftered and far too large for the task assigned it, that of corporeally correcting the skin of not so very terrible sinners of the fair sex. Its size alone struck awe into

our hearts, even if its appliances did not suffice for that task. There was a large fire, Miss Oakes sat on the edge of a worn deal table confronting us with three or four of the most ferocious canes I had ever seen behind her, and the Prefect stood beside our rank with her book. But all the furniture we could see was the board.

This simple affair was the guillotine in our lives of the moment. It was a plain upright board, or plank, resolutely accoutred with straps and bars, and for us it bespoke *pain*. We were going to have to bend over the board, buttocks bare, and be flogged.

The mistresses believed in variety. Some took the proceedings with many monitives; tonight Miss Oakes seemed averse to such. She merely nodded—"All right, Hutch, let's get on with it."

The monitor scrutinized her book. "Drayne?"

"Here."

"Tardy. Report of Miss Smith."

The mistress said, "Have you anything to say?"

"No, Miss."

"Do you wish to appeal?" On another negative Miss Oakes said simply, "Five. Take them off."

The girl, whom I did not know, was clearly used to the procedure. Her only visible signs of fear were certain grimaces of the mouth, as she gradually unbuttoned and undid her scant knickers and slid them off. As she went to one wall where we had to hang them on a hook, glimpses of alliciating white underbuttock could be seen. She was not a tall girl but had the same tantalizing liquid flesh of Georgiana, albeit fuller of form than she.

"Put her over tight."

With a much less certain look the girl approached

the board. She stood to it slightly astride and Hutchinson positioned her.

The feet went through two slots in the base, about half a yard apart. They were then securely stocked by bars behind the ankles. A further bar, adjustable at the knees, made any flexion of the legs impossible as well as undesirable. The top of the board came about hip-high, but contained a leaf which could be adjusted to various heights. Atop this was a leathern pommel against which you braced the pubis. Then an iron bar was adjusted just behind, in the small of the back; loosed on springs this bar then pressed there hard, cambering the loins, an effect all the more brilliantly produced as the monitoring Prefect then stood before the girl and, grasping her wrists, hauled her fully forward. Back curved, bottoms parted, tautened and arched out for the whip, the culprit was ready to suffer. And what a whip it was.

The Reverend Brocklehurst saw to it that nothing was spared in the severity of these occasions and the Duty rods were those employed with effect in boys' reformatories. Yellow, shiny, well-waxed their entire surface they were longer than the classroom canes and thicker at the tip, though almost as whippy. I was to learn what such minor modifications meant in intensification of suffering. A sound Duty flogging—and I was witnessing one—was something not even the hardiest girl wished to repeat in a term.

Bared by no more than a contemptuous flick of the cane under the skirt hem, the buttocks were well spread and stretched for treatment as the Prefect hauled on the culprit's arms from in front.

After stepping the soles of her shoes in some rosin at the side, the mistress measured aim and stood

back. She came about two paces forward, swinging; the sleek stick slickly divided the air with its drear whirr, then thumped into the underside of the cheeks, which it visibly drove upwards. The shock on the whole body attested to the gathered velocity of impact, while the involuntary squirm, and purple welt, affirmed its effect.

"One," said the Prefect loudly.

The mistress examined her weal. The girl in front of me ran her tongue on her lips. She was shaking. I caught her sick whisper, to herself, "Right in the crease."

There was a long pause whose silence was merely underlined by the quickened breathing of the sufferer, then two fell. A trifle higher, but a full-bodied blow.

The mistress said, "Damn!" Then, "Quite forward, please, Hutch." The third followed deep into the sulcal groove again and the girl gave a long exhaled "Ooooo-uuuuh!"

Her head came up between her shoulders and I could see her eyes tight shut. Fatty writhings of her inner cheeks, poor pathetic wrigglings of the wounded rounds together, spoke of her torment. She gave a short cry at the fourth but was silent after the fifth, her clenched mouth dribbling. The five thick weals flamed at the very bottom of her buttocks.

Miss Oakes looked appraisingly at these fat, blood-thickened welts drawn full across the underseat, for the Duty strokes were always delivered low, into the tender sulcus if possible. With a smile she unlatched the ankle-stocks and the legs shot back, threshing and writhing.

"All right." The Prefect released the sufferer from before and she jumped up, face crimson and con-

torted, grabbing at her inflamed flesh in rolls. The pain was mounting up in earnest now. She ducked a knee and mouthed an almost soundless "Thank you" to the mistress and then walked, or writhed, a-tiptoe to the side where she retrieved her scanty undergarment.

"Not bad, Jennifer," said the mistress. "You can get an A." And so the monitor duly inscribed it in the book, each of our official chastisements being graded for stoicism under the rod.

The girl made with ducked face to the door without putting on her knickers, as was the form. She looked thoroughly punished, through and through. Now it was the turn of pretty Teresa Palmer, up for four. A thin girl she went to her fate in demonstrable fear, whimpering at the board, "Oh Miss . . . please, Miss . . . oh please Miss." She cried lustily at the first but pulled herself together and endured three more thudding strokes with no more than panted gasps. She too was allotted an A. She writhed like a dervish on her way to the door, however.

Now poor Maud Morris, the answerer-back in the changing-room, was called forward. Her two faults were announced, she was sentenced to her awful eight, and she impassively peeled the thin fabric from her round bottoms. Bent over the board this was indeed an impressive rump, sturdy, well-parted, full of spring, with the afternoon's cuts clearly inscribed across the cheeks. Miss Oakes seemed to want to make sure the maximal severity permissible was inflicted, for any criticism of a mistress was conceived especially heretical.

She bounded forward and lashed the young chubs till they juddered again. Ferocious weals barred the

underneath proffered. With astonishing phlegm the girl silently reached six, after whose resounding whack she slowly stiffened, her cheeks squeezing in with her agony.

Like a runner at the end of a race she gasped back, "No, please . . . it is enough . . . dear God, to punish me so. . . ."

Miss Oakes smiled, watching the pain do its work.

"Relax," she said gravely. "Unclench them, Maud."

The girl groaned. The Prefect pulled her arms and the cane sang in again.

"Seven!"

"YOWWW!"

"Eight!"

"HOAAAW!"

Maud Morris writhed in perfect agony when it was over. She walked from the room slowly, holding herself and making dreadful deep groans.

"Next."

Wragg and Ponsonby were despatched in the same businesslike way and suddenly the room was whirling round me. I was there alone, facing the now slightly smiling mistress on whose upper lip I could see a droplet of sweat. It was happening, it was happening. . . .

"Eyre?"

"Here."

"Untidy. My report, Miss."

"Have you anything to say?"

"N-no, Miss."

I could not take my eyes from that frightful cane whose tip was pressing and bending at the floorboards before me.

"Wish to appeal?" On another negative the mistress then said, "First time?"

"Yes, Miss."

She nodded. "Three of the best. Take them off."

As I returned from hanging my miniscule knickers on the hook my beaten buttocks cringed in anticipation.

"Over tight, Hutch."

I was sick-throated as the monitor, first taking off my UNTIDY button, put me to the board. The leathern pommel came just to my height and, when I was pressed against it with skirt up in front, felt warm from the groins of the previous sufferers. My legs were stocked and straightened by the knee-bar. I bent over. Released across the small of my back the bar there, also padded with leather on its underneath, pressed most strongly. Its spring was very powerful, more so than I had expected and made me arch out my bottom behind. The Prefect then took my hands in hers. She did this by gripping my right wrist with her right, and I had to grasp hers back. Then the left was taken likewise, in her left, and with hands crossed over in this manner she hauled me forward. I realized I was on my toes and quaking all over.

The mistress examined her meat, feeling out the sulcal groove with a finger, since it was a tradition that the Duty cuts were delivered here where, any girl will tell you, it hurts most. Due to the friction of the overhang the skin is more tender at this point. Before I knew it I was cut.

"One," said the Prefect.

Ah, what a stroke! It fell with less sound than I'd expected but jolted me forward with a grunt. A savage wave of flame laved my lower person. Heavens,

how it stung. Suddenly, it seemed that a second wave rose and joined this first, mounting unbearably. I heard a breathless whine—my own—and cringed in my cheeks, so rudely assaulted. I held myself tense in spasm for what seemed minutes, then, exhausted, let my buttocks hang slack, and flaccid.

I was thumped again. This time I gasped aloud.

The monitor counted. The wave flamed. The pain ate in. Oh this was strict, indeed. The Duty cane doubled the agony. Again, a brief fury of rebellion helped me endure—it was unjust to be made to suffer so. Stocked, stripped, and given cuts to make a convict writhe, right in the tenderest part of our softest persons. But, where was the third?

"You're clenching," said the mistress.

"I cer-can't help it, Miss," I barely breathed.

"Well, you'd better or you'll get extra. Relax them quite now."

The third terrific stroke wrapped itself around me. I cried.

"One extra for clenching," I heard in the mists above my head and behind my bruised back.

It was given. I prefer to pass over what ensued. Somehow I managed to curtsey and leave that room. I was awarded but a C. What I best remember was the sudden access of pure white fire that attained me outside the door and sent me spinning like a dancer, grabbing great rubbery rolls of tormented flesh, in front of the grinning great girls there, as I tried in vain to pluck out the demon which was continuing to burn into and under my being.

"Hooouuu-aaaaah!"

"Tight enough for you, Eyre?"

"Why did you get four?"

"Feeling warm?"

I got to the dormitory and put myself to bed, as was the rule. Lying on my belly in the half-dark, I felt those brutal weals, the skin all hot and taut upon their bulges. I wished for the frame that birched girls were given, to raise the sheets off their flogged bottoms. The pain gradually dimmed, dulled and I felt warm all over.

Presently the door softly opened and closed and a figure approached me, that of Parker. Another was with her, the monitor's friend Crawford. Holding hands by my bed they looked down at me softly smiling.

"Bad luck, Eyre, we heard you got a Duty."

"A real beauty," said her friend, "according to Hutch."

"It did sting rather," I said with assumed bravado.

"Can we see them?"

"Oh all right," I said with a petulant shrug of my body.

My sheets were peeled down, my gown up and cool air calmed my buttocks.

"Phew! you certainly caught it on the right."

"You could put a ruler over the lot, I declare."

"Th-that one you're touching now," I said as a hand pulled the buttock slabs up to examine well under me, "that was the worst of all. The last one. For clenching."

I felt a curious quaint pride in having come through and in having these great girls examining my wounded person with such obvious respect.

"You should never clench with Oakes. She always notices," said Parker, still feeling me.

"Besides," added Crawford, "clenching only makes

it bruise more. It helps against the first sting, but not the second."

"It helps in birching, though."

"That's why they fig you first."

"What's that?" I asked.

"Ginger suppository up the anus. Makes you spread like billyho." The girls giggled, then Parker whispered something to her friend and Crawford left the room. The Dorm head leant over me and said a little breathlessly, "I'll put some cold cream on them for you, Eyre, and you'll feel ever so better, just you see."

I was not averse. Actually I was beginning to feel a pleasant heat in my soft and swollen lower lips. Parker went up to her alcove and came back and sat on my bed. She began to rub the cream into my cheeks with slow squeezing hands. I panted at once. Soon my hinds were so greasy they were slipping under her ministrations, blubbery balls of flesh that she churned together with her thumbs up their insides.

"Feel better?"

"Ooooh yes. Ber-but I . . . oh Parker . . . I'm. . . ."

She chuckled knowingly. "Relax. Let yourself go, silly." Then, "You'll have to cant your bum up a bit so's I can get at those lower weals."

With grateful greed I did so, on my knees, my loins arching of their own accord. I knew the twinned apricot of my sweet slot was pouching prettily back between the top of my thighs.

"Oh thank you," I panted. "This is lovely."

She laughed again and laved into my cunt with her greasy thumbs. I ooohed at once. I felt red-hot down there, like a kettle about to burst. When one thumb

flicked my clit I groaned aloud. The ready sentinel was stiff.

"I . . . oh heavens if you go like that . . . I'm, uigh, I'm afraid I'm going to squirt!"

"Of course you are," she chided. "Just let yourself go. You're learning something we all find out here sooner or later. It's five times as fine after a whipping. There, you're drippy as a sponge."

All the while she had been massaging the underside of my bud with the ball of her thumb. It was irresistible. I said quietly, "I feel I'm going to blow up now," and I did. She jammed her thumb full home, palming my belly, as I came, giving me purchase on which to mash my hungry red dragon. I jacked straight, gripping her wrist between my thighs, and tides of ecstasy flowed, molten, over me in wave on shaking wave. She was right. I had never known such lengthening of bliss, finger myself as I might at Gateshead. Finally, when I could look back limp, I saw Parker sniffing her hand with a smile.

"You smell of violets in a hot sun, darling," she said. "Heavens, you certainly go a lot. Was it good?"

I wriggled expressively for answer.

"Well, we shall have to wipe you off in the washroom, shan't we, or you will be on the mat for staining your sheets tomorrow. The grease won't matter so much, but if Matron sees your goo. . . !" She tugged at my shoulder. "Come on, idiot. Then you can be nice to me behind my curtain afterwards, can't you, I'm certain you've a tongue like an eel. Remember, I do have to give you three more in a mo'."

Suddenly I wanted to cry, and did so.

"Wha-wha-wha," I blubbered, keening. "We're

all always being caned here . . . and it hurts so much. . . ."

"Yes, but think what a lot of good it does you."

"Der-do you have to whip me again tonight, Parker?"

"Yes I have to but if you're very nice to me I'll try and take you highish. Anyway it's going to hurt like hell on the bottom you've got and if I let you off at all the other girls will notice, and guess. So I'll have to make them fairly tight ones but not too. How's that?" she asked me, grinning.

That night, after I had done to Parker what Eliza Reed had made me so proficient in, she gave me three blistering beauties before the grinning dorm and I went to bed in tears at her treachery as much as anything. With three more the next morning I would have had forty licks laid across my bottoms since the beginning of the week. This average of ten a day was not exceptional for new-knicks and I think Susan Cuningham had even surpassed it. But little did I know what Friday was to have in store for my poor bruised behind.

Whhhhhrppp!

EIGHT!

What a whistler!

Oh that I could only have stamped in my agony . . . but I was strapped strained, sweat pouring down the furrow of my back and into my peach-cleft below it. Dear God, how this man knew how to whip. My master, Edward Fairfax Rochester

"Ah God," I groaned when breath came back to me. "As you are merciful, sir, pardon me these last. . . ."

"But I am not merciful, Jane. You know that by now. And I am not because you do not want me to be."

He prepared for the next. . . .

8

"Angels see our tortures. . ."

Miss Temple had always something of serenity in her air, of state in her mien, of refined propriety in her language: never more so than when she read the Collect at morning prayers.

Friday was fine and fair. I felt a radiance throughout that morning whose source I did not know. Something of pride was in it when girls came up and asked if my Duty had been "tight." It had been, I assured them with a certain assumed nonchalance. I had

cleared the Untidy badge from my person, and, yes, *come through,* albeit with a C. I was one with them all now.

In a long vacant room in the pre-lunch break period someone was walking towards me in the mincing prance given by very high heels. It was the mistress Miss Miller, who had given me the "treat," one I had liberally repaid, or so it seemed to me. In my eyes now she looked lovelier than ever, as she fairly bounced forward, her tiny pleated tartan skirt flicking at the tops of her strong, round thighs. As she stood before me I could not keep from staring at the juncture of the latter. Behind the light material lay, I knew, a powerful, black-haired. . . .

"Jane Eyre!"

"Yes, Miss."

I stood there grinning before her, frankly trying to look my most winning, and pretty. After what seemed a long time, and without smiling, she said, "I think you will come to see me this afternoon at four."

My grin grew. Such an admonition from any other mistress would have been cause for my heart to drop into my shoes. But Miss Miller was my ally now. I felt I knew what she meant.

"Yes, Miss." And I ventured a slow wink.

She looked surprised and after another long while nodded to herself still unsmiling. "You don't understand, do you?" was all she said, as she strode strongly off, her skirt flipping on her round haunches behind. I could scarcely wait for those hours to pass. Finally four o'clock struck.

There was a good fire and everything in Miss Miller's room looked cheerful—if one kept one's eyes away from the canes. She herself was seated in a low

arm-chair on one side of the hearth and I saw at once that not only was she stockingless, she had nothing on beneath her tiny skirt. She lounged in such a way as to let me look at her great haired seam, and I looked.

"Will you take some tea, Jane?" she said solemnly.

"Oh thank you, Miss, thank you."

I dropped to my knees where the pretty tray had been placed on the little round table near the fire. How fragrant was the steam of the beverage which I poured myself while she watched—and the scent of the toast! Moreover, there was a good-sized seed cake, my favorite kind. As I cut myself a piece with her permission, I turned to say impulsively, "Oh Miss, it is so good to feel I have a friend, and that not every time I am summoned to a mistress's chambers will it be for personal chastisement."

I began to realize that Miss Miller had not moved a muscle since my entry, and that she was staring at me with a deep, unsmiling interest.

"I understand you got a Duty last night, Jane."

"Yes, Miss. Oh it hurt like anything. Would you like to see the marks?"

I stood up, treating her unthinkingly like a comrade and, I must admit it, hoping to seduce her by show of my invitingly plump bottom cheeks. I was indeed about to turn when I realized that her look was not one of interest so much as hostility.

"I begin to see that I was very wrong," she said slowly, at length. The teacup clattered as I set it down and my world started dissolving into the crumbs of the seed cake I equally shakily replaced.

"This morning I could scarce credit it that a new-knick like you imagined a mistress might become

your friend, but you seem to have truly got above yourself to this extraordinary extent, already. It is unbelievable. It reveals that you know absolutely nothing about the errand of Lowood, Jane Eyre. It is a *disciplinary academy.*" She almost shouted the last words at me. "You have probably heard that we mistresses get disciplined in turn for errors, and that our punishments make yours look like child's play—though no girl is ever granted to see one. Leniency to a pupil, any favoritism, is one of the worst offenses possible. I propose to eradicate it and drive from your mind once and for all the ideas you have evidently been entertaining there."

"Oh Miss, Miss. . . ." It was dreadful. I stood wringing my hands, close to tears again.

"First of all, failing to curtsey to me this morning and now, having the insolence to lower your eyes to my private person. For your own good, you are going to learn your place in life, Jane Eyre." She stood up and went to the side. "First let me show you something, though." She came back with a pencil and the school roll, neatly lettered. "Close your eyes and prick a name." When I had done so she said, "Good, a Major. Eileen Parsons. Do you know this girl?"

"Barely, Miss."

She strode to a bell-pull and tugged it. A maid appeared at once.

"Send Parsons," said the mistress and when the maid had gone she looked at me with, yes, literal loathing.

"I'm going to whip your buttocks as hard as I know how, Jane. And then I shall teach you your place. You'll not get three, you'll not get four, you'll

not get six. It's eight you're going to get, my girl."

"Oh Miss, mercy . . . I didn't mean . . . I never knew. . . ." I wrung my hands imploringly at her. "Oh I shall never be able to take so many, my behind is so sore. . . ."

"You will take them as well as this girl does or you will take them over, cut for cut, tied up in a Chastisement Chamber. Eileen Parsons has done nothing to merit punishment. She is a particularly meek and well-behaved girl whom none of us has been known to fault. Nevertheless, I shall flog her mercilessly and she will not complain, because that is the manner of Lowood. To be whipped by a mistress is a mark of esteem, a form of loving touching, do you understand? Now. I shall deal with you after you have watched her suffer. You will not need clothing. Strip to your shoes and then clear the center of the room of chairs so that I can get a good run at you both, and set the punishment table well against the wall."

I cried all the time I did so, utterly dismayed at how things had turned out and gone so topsy-turvy, and terrified of what was in store, a fear augmented by the juicy whistles of flourished canes as Miss Miller tested their pliancy on leather cushions.

Finally, I heard a knock.

A senior girl came in. Aged almost eighteen she was a trifle on the short side with thin flaxen hair, and a heart-shaped face with brown eyes. Her expression was solemn but impassive as she curtseyed, with barely a glance at my naked person, and the cane.

"You sent for me, Miss?"

Miss Miller's attitude towards this sultry senior

girl was quite different. She smiled and said, "Yes, I'm awfully sorry but I'm going to have to thrash you."

There was a brief silence, the girl's tongue ran over her lips, but her face did not change as she answered, "Very well, Miss. Now?"

"Yes. I don't think I've had this pleasure in quite a while."

"You gave me my last a year ago, Miss. Six of the best for talking in Prep."

"I'm glad you remember them, Eileen."

"Oh I do, Miss."

"Admirable. I want you to show this new-knick here how a great girl can take it. I need a model example. If you cannot provide me with it, Eileen, I shall have no hesitation in calling for the birch. Now then, roll up your skirt." When what there was of it had been so rolled, the mistress nodded. "Good. I like your buttocks. I shall not ask a senior girl like you to have to bare before a new-knick, therefore instead of six I shall give you eight, for the privilege of covering."

There was a pause. The girl frowned steadily at the floor.

"Miss. If I might be so bold."

"Yes?"

"I would willingly take them down and suffer the smaller count."

"For which unasked interjection I shall give you altogether nine."

"Yes, Miss"—after a moment.

"Bend over and put your bottom out, I'm beginning to feel you have not been beat enough, Eileen. So. Good. Jane Eyre, you come here."

In a lissom cat-like stretch the girl bent over the table at right angles, or a little more, her legs together. She was not secured, but a small gate in the form of a polished wood bar went behind her ankles and another at her knees, in front, so that her legs were effectively braced back; she reached right forward and buried her face between her arms, wreathed in her hair. A small flange in the table opened up and tilted at her groin.

I was made to kneel down close to her on the right, so that my face was at a level with her hips. Miss Miller took much pains to see that I was as close to the part to be punished as possible—"And don't take your eyes off for a second, Jane." By the time she had finished positioning me my nose was almost on the outstretched part and she laughed and said, "If I hit your face, I'll let you off it all. Meanwhile, just look and concentrate on your nothingness."

I had before my fearful gaze, then, the peerless silken rounds of Eileen Parsons, all too soon to be punished—for nothing. They were clad in the transparent skin of the Major's knickers, white with pale blue satin ribboning. At Lowood one learnt that God made us each separate individuals, and that each bottom is different.

This was a lovely one, nicely fatted yet not too much so, with little overhang; what they were remarkable for was their strong deep young separation, each cheek seemed to stand out proudly on its own. There was a sudden whizz of yellow before my eyes and I blinked and recoiled. The first slice had fallen. It was a beautiful blow, visibly lifting the chubby flesh. Miss Miller turned and strolled back.

There was a profound silence. The mistress was taking about three paces to her run and, after what seemed a long time, she bounded forward again and gave her target another full-bloodied swipe that seemed to shave my nose by inches—*whuck!*

"Keep your eyes open, Jane Eyre."

"Yes, Miss."

These first two were the "sighting" strokes, full across the arse cheeks, one about an inch or more above the other. The mistress would now try to place the rest of the count in between these darkening bands, visible beneath the stretched cambric, to produce, if she were accurate of aim, a single solid aching lump of unbearable burning pain. And—*whuck!*—the third now drove surely in, right between the pair. Eileen Parsons shifted her feet, but gave no other sign. I ventured a timid glance as the mistress strode back this time; a pleat of her skirt had caught in her cleft, behind, and with awe I saw her thick round thighs and the bulge of buttock cheek, so much wider and fatter and more powerful than her victim's. Soon I was to suffer too . . . ah God, give me strength.

She lounged back, one hand on hip, taking her time. The first three fearful swipes had taken perhaps a minute. They meant a mounting toll for the girl whose first symptoms of suffering I, set so close, could now discern, a fleshy writhing-in at the base of the cheeks which were surprisingly downy. The mistress came for her fourth. Her skirt swung and I saw the thickly tufted bush which looked to me, in my present state of terror, large and cruel. She swung so hard now I heard her grunt. Still the stoical girl made no sign. After the fifth there was another long

wait and I stole a glance along the table-top. The girl had turned her face between her arms, to my side; her forehead, quite crimson, was contorted and she was biting into the top of her right arm, at the shoulder, so as to help to bear the pain.

Perhaps the relentless mistress noticed my glance for she said slowly, "Am I hurting you, Eileen?"

Forced to answer, the girl brought up her head and hissed out an eloquent, "Yesssssss!" She raised up on her arms—"Please, Miss, mer-mer-may I have a rest? I have not been beat like this for some time and I had forgotten how dreadfully it stings. Ooooh!"

Miss Miller laughed mirthlessly. "All the more reason to whip you often. Right over now, please."

After the sixth she again gave a long pause. The cheeks were terribly bruised by now. She was clearly growing excited, breathing hard and flushing.

"Three more," she said thoughtfully—and delivered them, three of the most unbelievably punishing thrashes I had ever seen, with the whole weight of her body behind each and small interval between. Then she stood well back with a gasped, "All right." Then she added, "Unlatch her ankles, Jane."

Eileen Parsons reacted with strange somnambulistic slowness. She had taken the last two risen a little and now straightened to her full height with a drawn-out gargle or slow retch of pure agony, mounting in tone, as if about to vomit—"Aaaargggggugh!"

Her wealed cheeks jammed together as if suddenly clutching something between them and she grabbed them in handfuls with her hands. But her face was what drove the marrow from my bones. It was crimson in hue all over, martyred in expression, and in the dribble on the chin were flecks of blood. She

turned and tottered, as if scarce able to credit the extent of pain accorded her.

"You may go now, Eileen. Well done."

The girl doubled in agony—"Oouuuuu! Owwww! Ah God oh God. . . ." She seemed unable to see where she was, took two faltering stiff steps, then straightened like a marionette in another drawn-out spasm. Her right arm was freely bleeding where she had bitten into it. I gazed in open horror. My turn next. Finally, the poor thing found the door like some spastic but could not wrench the handle open. She ducked down, perhaps an attempted curtsey, said, "Th-thank you, Miss," finally found strength to open the door and staggered out.

Miss Miller was staring at me. I remember thinking that her dilated nostrils looked twice their width. Oh heavens, how frightened I felt. She was staring at me in a dazed way, almost dreamily, and finally she shook herself, saying, "I can't remember when I have ever given three better cuts than those last ones. Mr. Brocklehurst himself could not do better. Don't you think they hurt her tremendously, Jane?"

"Tremendously, Miss," I echoed faintly.

Still in the same trance-like way, she set down her stick and came towards me. Then this strange whimsical woman put an arm about me and my head on her breast; I could hear her heart throbbing under the lump of easily moving tit. When she spoke it was almost mournfully:

"And now I am going to have to teach you your place in life, am I not, Jane Eyre? How you are the lowest of the low. Scarce fit to drink my urine, which you will do every day next week. There will be a

carafe on the side and you will take your dose from it daily, and gladly. The constituents are no more than those of beef tea, with a little uric acid added. Yes, yes, you will begin to learn your role in life and that when a mistress tells you to keep your eyes on a behind, you will do so and not look under her skirt. Oh yes, I saw you, mischief. And every one of your cuts will be as hard as those last three, or harder if I can make them."

I had begun to cry again. "I shall never be able to bear them, Miss," I whimpered.

"Oh yes you will, for if you do not it's the Chamber, tied up like a parcel and the whole over. But for you, Jane, since you are nice and tender behind, I shall use a thin cane, the thinnest that I have, no more than a pencil in thickness. They are hard to find these days. The bruise is less but the sting far more intense, more especially when I take you among your bruises and slice up. Oh it will snip in here, and here. . . ." She started to feel me.

I blurted impulsively, "Ah Miss, I love you . . . please, I didn't mean. . . ."

She thrust me imperiously from her and to my dismay I saw I had turned her into fury again. A new Megaera. I was in despair.

"Incorrigible minx. Do you mean to seduce me, too? Bend over that table and let me show you what a cane whipping can be." And she went to the wall for her rod.

It was, indeed, an unspeakably stingy one and its infliction atrocious. I stood three, a count I was growing accustomed to by now, but dashed my hands back at four. At five I had to be corrected again. I was by now terribly tender behind and each slice

seemed to me like a knife. After a frightful sixth, endless in coming, I stood up—"Aaaah! It's no good, Miss, I can't bear more."

It was the truth. "Bend over at once," was my reply, given with venom in the voice.

Indeed I tried. I was half-over when the seventh lashed me with its streak of fire. I screamed and sat down on the carpet, tripping back on the ankle-bar. I lay there, moaning desperately as I kneaded myself, and looking up at the giantess—for so she seemed—with the great–haired gash beneath her skirt who towered over me.

"Foolish girl! You will see I keep my promises."

She strode to a bell-pull. A maid came at once.

"Elsie. Take this child and if you can find one of the Chastisement Chambers free put her in position four. I mean to show her that a punishment can be taken calmly."

The maid looked pleased. "Yes, Miss. Punishment corset too?"

"A notched saddle, Elsie. And the pear. Take your time. I shall be along to cane her shortly." She looked down at me in disgust. "By the time Elsie's finished with you, Jane, you won't be able so much as to twitch. Off with you now."

"I think I'll just get some straps first, Miss, if I may."

The smiling maid went to a drawer, took out some evil-looking straps of hard thin leather, and approached me as I sat, nursing my wounds.

"Come," she coaxed, as one might address a pet—and then she indeed secured my neck in a pretty, ornate dog collar, attached to a leash which she held in her hand. I rose to my feet, sobbing brokenly.

"Ah please, Miss, please . . . I tried, I did try. . . ."

"Not hard enough," was the implacable answer.

There was a ring in front of my collar, and a ring behind, and a ring in front of the belt I was buckled into, and a ring behind that also. Then I watched in dismay as a severe round long leather leash was clipped to my collar in front. This was passed down through my front belt ring, brought up between my legs, being carefully threaded through my lips there, up through the belt ring behind, and then passed through the collar ring behind also. My wrists were cuffed and raised high behind my back and the leash clipped tautly to them there. I gasped at the tension. This was the first "saddle" (as we termed them at Lowood) I had worn, though I had seen them applied to other girls already, who seemed to suffer atrociously whenever bending or sitting in them.

I soon realized that my ignoble harness was such that unless I strained my arms back until they seemed to leave their sockets, my wrists exerted pressure on the leash—and I felt as if I were being cut in half under the cunt. As the glossy-faced, raven-haired maidservant then tugged me forward like a dog in this way, my head went back with a gasp; what fiends had devised this way of vexing girls? For the part of the leash that passed through my sex was rather thicker and lumpier and the leather on its inside must have been roughened in some manner, for it greatly abraded the tender flesh up which it rode. Never had anyone trod more like Agag, "delicately."

"Curtsey," smiled the maid at the door. She had a switch in her hand.

I looked desperately back at my place of martyr-

dom. For some reason the mistress was holding her head in her hands. I went down slowly on one knee —and squeaked! The lozenge of rough leather positively seemed to bite.

Outside the door at last the maid hurried me briskly along the corridors to the Chastisement Chamber.

"Please, Elsie," I begged. "Not so fast. This strap is cutting awfully."

"Oh that's nothing. I'm going to put a far more interesting one on you in a minute, just you see."

A mistress was coming towards us. It was Oakes.

"Curtsey," I heard. I did. And gasped. It bit again.

"Good Heavens!" said the mistress, standing with hands on hips and grinning for all she was worth. "What have we here?"

"I'm just taking her along to a Chamber for a proper hiding, Miss," said the maid.

"Poor Jane Eyre. Didn't I hurt you enough last night?"

"Yes, Miss."

"She got some lovely licks from Miss Miller, Miss. Look." Elsie turned me and they both admired my streaked cheeks.

"I wish I knew where Miller got those thin canes," said Miss Oakes. "But let's see what I gave you. Bend over now."

"Please, Miss. . . ."

"What is it?"

"It hurts so to, in this."

Then I squeaked again, only louder. With a laugh the maid thrust me over by the scruff of my neck. Miss Oakes palped my welts of the previous night. When I stood up again she was shaking her head,

"Dear me. I thought I'd hit you hard enough to keep you out of mischief for a day or two. Ah well, the perils of education, I suppose."

She went her way.

"Curtsey again!" said that grinning devil to me, and I had to. Oddly, as we walked on, I was becoming flooded with contradictory sensation; partly it was the constriction, partly the warmth of retiring pain, and partly the leather lump below, which, smoother at the top, would insist on rubbing at my stiffening sentry there.

There were four Chastisement Chambers for the use of the mistresses at Lowood, at any time, and each was gloomier than the other. Truly they were more fitting for the Inquisition than for the care of girls like us. Roomy and vaulted, they were equipped with every imaginable appurtenance of restraint and correction. Directly she had closed the massy door on mine, the maid put me to a corset yard, my arms high raised and secured at the wrists. There was a cheval glass before me in which I could see myself. At least the harness was off.

"Thank heavens for that, Elsie," I said; "that strap was a demon. Oh merciful God, I can never take another cut, as tender as this behind."

"Just you wait," she said merrily, busying herself to one side. "By the time I've trussed you up, you'll take your cuts like a soldier. Without a move and without a single sound. For I have to gag you, first. You've never had the pear, eh?"

I confessed I had not. She came forward and showed me the infamous choke-piece with its strong spring, for the jaw muscles are among the strongest in the body. When she had closed the pear against

the spring, it looked like a small crab apple made of lead. When opened, it would hold my mouth splitting wide, so that I could not utter a sound.

"First we'll flavor it for you, shall we," she said with a giggle.

"No, you don't have to," I begged, knowing.

She smiled and then spat on the frightening object. "Some of us only dip it in," she said, moving ominously behind me. "But I like to put it right up. Like that it always collects some stuff, you see. And it won't be the first you'll taste here at Lowood, I assure you."

"Noooooouuuh!"

I squirmed as the now slobbery pear was introduced up my rectum. I felt it slip up the sheath, quite high, and said, "Oh please. I shall never be able . . . to expel it, Elsie."

"Yes, you will. Unless it should spring open in your insides. Just think of that." This terrifying idea sent her into another fit of merriment. "But that's never happened yet. Now then. Like a glass of water before we start?"

Never had well water tasted purer than that cold cup given me then. The maid powdered my torso completely. Her gloved hands, over which the soft leather stretched so tightly every indentation of her finger-nails might be seen, caressed me knowingly.

"You've a lovely plump body, haven't you?" she crooned as she did so. "Just fit to be thrashed into, down here."

I was beginning to cry again. "But I'm whipped so often, Elsie. And I don't want to be."

"But you're going to be, aren't you? Some more lovely violet lines back here."

"Do you like seeing me, seeing us, whipped so much?"

"But of course," she answered, genuinely startled. "And so will you, silly, by the time you finish at Lowood. You'll be fairly longing to send little girls up for Yellows. Now let's get a nice tight corset."

It was a vise. To this day I shall swear that those punishment corsets were lined with iron. The one Elsie put on me as I puffed and dangled was short, and accoutered with thin straps. It finished under my breasts, practically cracking my ribs there, and it took my tummy away so that I could barely breathe at all. The maid worked like a veritable farrier about my body, tugging the laces and kneeing into me behind for greater leverage on them. I protested, panting, in vain. She used special tools with hook-ends to further tighten the stays. Finally, when I was a solid leathern tube from rib-cage to hips, she came and stood in front of me, her pretty face tilted: "I'm sorry to have to do this to you, y'know, but it's the only way to get them tighter."

"But they woooooon't . . . ," I feebly began, only to feel every atom of breath belted from my body. The maid had swung her fist into my belly and for a second I was an empty balloon, fighting for air, for existence itself. I dangled slackly. In this state I was easily notched in tighter. When I came to something of myself, the air seemed red and smelling salts were pressed to my nostrils.

"Now let's get that little toy out of you, shall we?" I heard.

The yard was lowered. I found my feet. It was lowered further still.

"Squat," she said, "and void it out of you quite."

I found it surprisingly easy to do so, into the large pan Elsie placed between my legs for the purpose. The corset so held me in its iron grip that I felt no control of my lower person at all. No sooner had I squatted slightly than of its own volition I felt the hellish pear sliding out of me; it fell with a loud clang into the pan—which seemed much to amuse the maid—and then I was gasping hectically, "Elsie . . . please . . . I can't help it . . . I'm going to do some more."

I thumped a large, warm one into the waiting pan and then it was upon me, I felt it coming, and there was *absolutely nothing I could do about it at all.* The hot gush came out of me, too, of its own accord and foamed into the pan.

"Heavens, what a jet!" exclaimed Elsie. And she grinned when she removed the pan from behind me —"I've not seen a better head on Dortmund larger."

When she came back from disposing of it it she stood before me and she was not smiling. She held up the slimy choke-pear. "You squeezed a bit of muck into it, new-nick, and like that you'll taste your waste while the mistress flogs you and shows you your true position in life, and not to be lippy with your betters."

The horror was duly introduced and sprung. My jaws widened to total distension. And there I stood, facing the stranger in the mirror—gape-mouthed, purple-faced, lily-skinned and bisected by the glossy black corset, a wasp of waist whose hips looked twice their size. And then the fun started in earnest.

Two thin straps sliced into my creamy shoulders, suspendering the cruel corset there. After this, there was threaded through my legs from the busk in front

the most fiendish saddle strap imaginable; it was thin and hard and lined with brass studs on the inside. It was hauled up so excruciatingly tight at the buckle behind that I saw myself blink and heard myself choke.

Elsie said slowly: "If you feel yourself retching, breathe in deeply. But you need not worry. A girl can vomit through a pear quite easily; besides there's the nose. However, you may get extra cuts if you do."

She swung me to get that awful strap still tighter, and last made me draw my knees up to my chest and hold them there, while she yanked mercilessly. When I lowered my legs again, my eyes started with the agony. Tears formed and flowed down my cheeks.

"There. What did I say? Like that you won't want to clench, will you. It gives them a lovely spread behind." She let me off the yard. "Come on, I love putting a girl to a Four."

I tottered, rather than walked, spraddle-legged to another part of the room, where a large 4 was inscribed atop a post set in the wall, and furnished with many more straps. I was bent absolutely double against this, head on knees, and trussed like a turkey. First, my arms were strapped at wrist and above and below the elbows, the lean leather cutting into my flesh painfully. My arms were then drawn up vertically behind me, doubling me quite, and secured by more straps to the wall-post there—at wrist, elbow, and with two more new straps holding my shoulders. My legs were strapped at ankle, above and below the knee, and at mid-thigh. My ankles were gyved immovably in a fetter that protruded from the wall and held them locked about a foot from it. Lastly, a de-

vice was screwed out from the wall at my knees. This was a double bar, padded with leather, and it was adjusted to push back at my legs just above and below the knee-cap. It was tightened so as to be almost intolerable. My legs were braced in a bow, my body was constricted and doubled till I couldn't breathe, my mouth was gagged—I was so helpless I did not exist. It was true to say that my whole feeling towards my body was altered in this position; I couldn't contract a single muscle of my buttocks or legs, they belonged to someone else, inert and divided by the cruelly biting thong one stud of which had eased into my anus.

Elsie administered the restorative salts once more, said "Don't run away" with a chuckle and again advised me to breathe deeply after each cut.

Presently the door opened and Miss Miller came in. I saw her from upside down as she came up to me, holding the same thin cane.

"Is she nice and taut, Elsie?" she asked.

"As a drum, Miss. I think she'll be able to take this lot without moving at all."

"Good gracious, her face is as red as her bum. Did you season the pear for her first?"

"Oh yes, Miss. She's tasting it nicely."

"And will swallow a bit when she gulps, eh? Good. Now. Where do you think I should cut in order to make it hurt most—on these last ones?"

"Yes, Miss, they're lovely. But frankly I think she's going to feel it almost anywhere like this. It's a fine thick pair to work on."

"Just sponge them for me first, will you. I like 'em wet for these very thin canes."

I felt the water slide with curious humiliation over

my beaten flesh; tears began to stream reciprocally over my suffocated upper cheeks. Miss Miller stood well back and doffed her high-heeled shoes. As she came forward swinging, her skirt again flared up and I saw her strongly haired slot. Then there was the yellow flash, the meaty thump, and a goddess drew a white-hot iron on my bum. She cut excruciatingly low and the pain seemed double that I had suffered in her room. I wanted to jump a yard away, succeeded in raising my heels from the floor with a deep belly-grunt of pure agony. I heard Elsie say calmly, "Good shot, Miss." I snorted snot.

Two fell in total silence, and three. Impossible to describe the pain I was in. After an endless interval—*four!*

The maid said, "I think you're hurting her nicely now."

"I'm trying to. It's all she understands. Sponge her down again, would you."

After the infernal sixth Elsie said, "You've drawn, Miss."

"Good heavens, I believe I have. A graze at least. It's been years since I drew with a cane."

"You're getting beautifully inside the cheeks, too, Miss."

"That's because you spread them so nicely for me, Elsie. Now then, let's see if I can just split that tip-mark with one of these last two."

"Split it like a plum, Miss, and she'll never forget it."

When that living hell was over I heard the mistress talking in the red mists above me, the scarlet pain waves laving my loins, my whole being. She was saying thoughtfully, "Give her ten minutes like that, put

some pimentade on that graze, and then bring her to me. That was good exercise."

She left. Before she went to get the stinging stuff, the maid said, "There now. You see, you took that beating perfectly stoically, didn't you?"

When eventually I was returned to the mistress's private room, from which I had first issued, it was merely at leash's end and with my wrists secured behind me. I was completely cowed and overpowered. Something in me had given up. The sting in my buttocks still sung through me from that lancinating lashing. All I knew was that I wanted the world to come to an end.

After I had curtseyed I looked glumly up and saw Miss Miller standing in the middle of the room with her legs apart. She looked flushed of face, which was fulfilled, almost sated in expression, yet still deeply hostile, and she was holding a thin cravache.

"There," said Elsie, "she's much better now, Miss."

"Do you think she knows her place?"

"Oh yes, Miss, I'm sure she does."

"We'll see. Come here, Jane Eyre."

I stood before her.

"Still feeling above yourself?"

"Oh ner-no, Miss," I quavered.

"Very well. I shall now show you your true relationship to a mistress. We have discussed the scum buss, have we not? I shall accord you the privilege of giving me one now. Kneel down behind me, after you have first lifted my skirt behind, and then get it right up, mind."

I went behind her. There being no other method to complete her order I bent and caught up the hem of her morsel of skirt in my teeth and laid it on the

arch of her crupper. The woman's body was lightly quivering and smelt hot. Kneeling behind her well-spread legs I saw she had affixed sharp round rowel spurs to each ankle. The superb buttock mass before me was supremely *there;* for a giddy second the room seemed full of arse. The cheeks were fully fatted and I had to push in with my face between them, to reach the crinkled rose-coin. I found the damp medallion, pressed with the tip of my tongue and sank it forward, half-smothered in rich thick bum flesh.

"Further up than that," I heard, as if from some mellow distance. "Get it right clean up."

I was held to the filthy task for a good ten minutes. I heard Miss Miller say, "There, Elsie, don't you think that's her real position in life? You may go now but be ready to come back at once if I want you."

"I shall be right outside the door,"—and then I heard it slam.

After a little wriggling, Miss Miller drew away and addressed me with intense dislike—"Well, girl, did you feel anything? Is there something up there, then?"

"I der-don't . . . I can't say, Miss," I stammered breathlessly.

"Try again then."

I set myself once more to the abominable task and this time, after some minutes, was able to reply to the resultant catechism—"Yes, Miss, I think there is s-s-something there."

"Good. Now come here." She led me, licking my bitter lips, to one side of the fire where a chair had been set out in a special way, with a towel on its seat. My heart failed me. The human cushion! I had come to this already. It was one of the vilest degradations we could be subject to.

Miss Miller was looking at me gravely, holding my trembling chin in her free hand.

"You know what a brown nose is, Jane Eyre?"

"Yes, Miss."

"You're now going to get one. Yes, I shall condescend to teach you your real role in life, my child. Sit down in front of this chair, put your head back on the cushions and your knees high." These last were secured by straps provided therefor, to the armrests of the comfortable chair. My cunthole yawned wide spread. "Now then, Jane Eyre, you will get your nose up where your tongue has been and keep it there, for as long as I choose. If you do not, you will feel the braided trainer of this switch in your most sensitive spot. I shall use the spurs on you without mercy. First, you will need this. For I shall grant you the favor of breathing, you see, though every now and then you may have to inhale my other insides, as I choose." She put a red tube in my mouth and, after settling a hassock before the chair, bestrode me; my being shook, my breasts trembled. My head was back, expectant. My arms were secured behind me and my bent legs parted. All I could see, think of, imagine was the great mass of buttock-cheek bunched above me. Then, holding the arm rests of her chair, the mistress descended her huge hams on me. The hinds parted, lushly forested within; I saw their insides somewhat flabbily approaching, and then I saw no more.

Wettened by my tonguing, the sphincter dimple opened on my nose at once, engulfing it deeply. Then as the whole weight of the massive mistress was lowered on me I panicked—was I to be suffocated alive in my first week at Lowood? I wriggled uselessly and

squirmed in earnest as the spurs roweled me unsparingly right inside my thighs. The two halves of perspiring flesh obliterated everything. My eyeballs felt pressed back, my entire face was enclosed in the gluteal globes. I found I could just breathe through the tubing. The mistress put her feet up, to increase the weight, and appeared to be reading a book. Every now and then she made fatty stirrings, which sent a repulsive ooze over my face, the while she would grind her hairy pulp into my chin. Truly I thought to faint. My tears added salt to the bile.

How I wish I could say, gentle reader, that it was the only exusion that I felt there. Alas, after some half hour of this stupefying cushioning in sheer arse-flesh, the mistress saw fit to lean forward and frankly excite herself. She put her book down and frotted herself frantically, coming in strong spurts that she verily mashed into me. I tasted of this unseemly essence, too, as I sucked through the tube.

Perhaps an hour went by thus, possibly two. Gross blots of darkness floated in my eyes. Twice I thought to faint. Waves of lethargic flatulence passed into my nostrils, and over my face, from the relaxed sphincter. And then I felt it pinch me. I all but panicked as I realized what was happening. The mistress leant forward with a satisfied grunt, a pose in which I could better hear her voice, and I felt something solid sliding down the steamy, slippery aisle above me. At the same time, leaning well forward, Miss Miller insinuated a finger in my slot and busily rubbed up my button there. I responded at once, helplessly. My tension made my excitement intense. The dread mass was emerging—fortunately short, and firm—and

then it was being smeared over me by the mistress's movements.

"There, Jane, there," she was saying, as she made contented, catlike stretching of her bum-cheeks. "You repulsive little detail. You filthy object. *That* will show you your true place in life, here at Lowood, and I beg you never to forget it, else I will order you the birch until your skin is crimson. Now, now. Yes, you filth, you will go tonight to the kennels—though not before Parker has given you your nightly three—and you will not wash your face until tomorrow. It will be in your nostrils and you will breathe it all the night. There, there. You are coming . . . admit it!"

Admit it, I had to. The spurs dug, the foul turd was slowly mashed over my abused countenance—and I gave to my tormentress endless gouts of gismic glue. Thus was I "shown my place," "brought down a peg or two," by ardent Miss Miller.

Thhhwwwrlllp!

NINE!

Ye Gods, what mortal agony.

"Aiyyyyy" *I cried aloud.*

Mr. Rochester had never hit harder. He had prepared his meat perfectly by the first strokes and could now take his time and cut into solid welt, fast oozing on the right.

I twisted back my tear-wet face and again begged him, "Mercy, sir. But come at me higher for these last three."

"Why should I, Jane, if it hurts more lower?" he amicably answered and stood back to complete his hellish handiwork on my person.

I sank my head between my shoulders, sweat streaming down my back under the lights, and tried to remember Lowood. . . .

9

My first quarter at Lowood seemed a century; and not the golden one, either. It comprised a most irksome struggle with difficulties in habituating myself to new rules and unwonted tasks. The fear of failure constantly harassed us, the threat of the whip was ever present—though it diminished in frequency, if not in intensity, with seniority.

At the end of that first, so frightful week, we were

received by Miss Temple and all the mistresses in their common-room. It was Sunday after chapel and an august and imposing moment for us four trembling new-knicks. The Headmistress presided at the head of a table, wearing a short pretty plaid cloak and her usual agreeable smile. We always had to prosternate ourselves in her presence, head on floor, and remain thus until bidden to rise. We were lectured long and intimately. Miss Temple urged us to endure all, to keep our spirits up and to march forward "like stalwart soldiers." I, for one, felt much too dejected to respond to this advice; and Estella Moore, standing next to me, was crying openly, her behind being in like state to mine.

But with what pride did we not all on the following Monday morning don the new rosy knickers of the Minimus class to which we were thus graduated! At last the dormitory cuts ceased and it seemed to me that Parker looked on me, at least, with a more friendly eye. We were part of the school and soon formed "chums" and "pals." A week later I had the pleasure of seeing my first public birching, the first of many I was to witness under the grim roof of Lowood.

I say *pleasure* with intent for such I must aver it to be, as such it was to become, ere I left that mansion. For the sterile rote of class and commons soon came to condition its inmates to rejoice at any disturbance within it. Furthermore, these whippings were exciting on other scores: they were excruciatingly painful, almost on another level than any other applications to which we were subject, and they were happening to *somebody else!* Add to this the fact that they took place in the mid-morning break period after which all

further classes were suspended for the rest of the morning, and you will recognize, gentle reader, the buzz of animation with which their knowledge was greeted amongst us.

"There's to be a flogging!"

This whisper, at breakfast, set faces flushing, elbows nudging, eyes sparkling. Two girls had evidently been caught in bed together, after Lights Out. Wagers were taken on the count to be allotted and we stole glances around to see which of our number were missing, for any girl to be birched was put into Solitary until expiation.

The infliction was carried out in the Long Chamber or refectory, in front of all the mistresses, who sat on the dais, Miss Temple in their center, and the assembled school ranged along the three remaining walls, as to the Minimus class facing them, Majors on the right, Minors on the left. The monitors faced inward to these three classes, until punishment commenced. The block was in the middle, and every eye was upon it. Even to this day I cannot write of it without trembling fingers, so unspeakably did those birch-twigs flick and sting, for minute after minute. They were prolonged, ferocious thrashings and you felt the weals for a week.

During the break period Miss Temple usually made announcements, said a few prayers, and dismissed us. However, she also ordered punishments which were administered publicly, before us. There were usually reports of some Prefect who wished a girl to get more than her class share of cuts and "put in" for such. The girl had to stand out, her offense was read and she was asked if she had aught to say. On the conventional negative she bent double after

dropping her knickers, her skirt was lifted, and the white-clad Duty Prefect of the day duly administered six terrific swingers "of the very best." If the Pre' (as we called her) failed to send the girl back to her ranks other than gasping and gripping her bottom, in literal agony, she had not performed ardently enough, and—so it was rumored—would be accordingly rewarded by the Duty Mistress that evening. Meanwhile, in front of all her colleagues and comrades, the victim strove amain to show no signs of pain. It was a veritable duel between them, one nearly always won by the wielder of those wicked rods. There were one or two great big Yorkshire girls who could "swallow" a sixer without blinking, but they were rare; and however they hid it, they were still ablaze beneath when it was over, like any one of us.

There were other orders also, during these break periods. I well remember that regularly every birthday I would see Miss Temple smiling gently towards me from her lectern on the dais: "Stand out, Jane Eyre. Today is Jane Eyre's birthday and her Aunt Reed wishes her to have cuts." And I would receive a tart "present" from that horrible woman of six stingers on my bum.

"I am sorry to have to say," Miss Temple began on the particular day in my first half that I mention, "that two among you have been caught in a disgusting sin and shall have to be punished severely. Bring in—" and she read out two names, only one of which was known to me. The Duty Prefect went to a door behind our rank and opened it to lead in two sorry penitents, both bare-footed and completely nude, with arms fettered wrist-to-elbow behind, and round each neck a small sign hanging—TRIBADISM. After

prosternation these two luckless girls stood facing the dais for their sentencing.

They could not have been more contrasted. The older of the pair, whose name I did not know, was nearer a woman. In her last term at Lowood, already spoken for as a governess in Lincolnshire, she was shorter than her younger accomplice in crime, with reddish-brown hair cut short and an appealing, rather pretty face. Her rich, close-curled bush was auburn, too. Her figure was unusual in the extreme. Her shoulders were gently sloping, her waist narrow, her legs normally tapering; but her stout bottom was wide to the point of deformity. It was not a long buttock, like that of Helen Burns, it was, rather, a short, strong, stocky one, surpassing in breadth of base any I had seen. The roll of fat at the overhang was solid and already somewhat tumified-looking. I could not help feeling a sense of satisfied anticipation at seeing this broad-arsed girl I did not know waiting for it, as we all had to; it was also rumored she was a well-known seducer of younger girls for such pleasures, and that there had been some rivalry with her dormitory monitor in the matter. She seemed to have resigned herself to her fate and, though not quite as impassive as a soldier, her crupper seemed to me a "stalwart" one. It shone a rosy hue on the right, where Neil had pre-treated it; for all girls due for the birch had to lie on a bed while the massive, flaxen-haired housekeeper applied hot towels to their rumps and then pumiced the cheeks with a pumice-stone until the integument sometimes felt so thin a finger-nail's touch would have split it.

The other girl was called Jessica Cameron and was exceedingly pretty and slim, with sleek dark hair;

her whiter bottoms trembled like jellies before our eyes all through Miss Temple's long peroration on their sin. She was clearly terrified of her ordeal.

We were all breathlessly awaiting the sentencing and, I confess, hoping that for the older girl it would be a tolerably strict one. Neil had told us two or three dozen was the usual rule, so that the final verdict was met with no less than a mild susurration of surprise round that long chamber.

Speaking slowly but sternly to the older girl, Miss Temple said: "As the chief culprit here in this disgraceful matter, you will bend over the block and your naked buttocks will be flogged forty-eight times with the birch twigs." Four dozen! "Further, you will then receive ten stripes of the martinet, also on your naked buttocks. You will suffer two days in Solitary and three hours of Detention. You, Cameron, will also bend tight your bottom and you will receive thirty-six strokes of the birch-rod, followed by five with the martinet. Let this be a lesson to you. Proceed with the punishment."

As the senior girl advanced with a curtsey to the block I could see she looked a little dismayed. This excruciating additive of strokes with one of our knotted cord martinets, falling on flesh that resembled that of some skinned rabbit, was, I later learnt, a recent directive or encouragement from the ever-thoughtful Mr. Brocklehurst, who felt we did not suffer hellishly enough on such occasions and were in danger of growing "soft."

Neil, who had been supervising the buckets of birches, came forward with the "fig," or caustic anal suppository. This foul thing was supposed to discourage us from clenching during cuts; it burnt horribly

and had the effect, on me at least, of making my sphincter open and shut involuntarily. It was administered to the girl bending over, then she straightened and Neil kept her finger fully up to drive it home and let it melt for a minute or more, the while the girl had every eye upon her. She was then put to the block by the two accessories of the administration, black-leathered Neil and the Duty Pre' in white.

"Miss Hall, the first dozen, please."

The young undermistress, tall and blonde, looked obviously pleased to have been chosen for the all-important first dozen, as she bowed gracefully to Miss Temple and stepped down off the dais, her tiny skirt swinging. The arse she approached, with a slight smile, was certainly a regal one, spread out for her ministrations. The girl's knees were nicely apart, her shins secured at ankle in the shallow troughs for them on the ledge. Straps also bound her knees into the block, which she gave the odd impression of clasping since her arms were secured either side of it, at elbow and wrist. Her upper body then fell well forward over the transverse slope which, alas, I must relate had a serrated surface in its ebon wood. The culprit was forced to gain purchase with her palms at the sides to push her chest up off these points, thus arching strongly in the celebrated "anvil" pose beloved of birchers. For it was an important element of the ceremony at Lowood that the sinner's face should be seen by all; I cannot express how dismaying and discouraging it was to see a great girl one admired with starting eyes and crimson cheeks after a couple of dozen. To this end Neil was now tying back the girl's hair.

I felt a nudge and the silly girl at my side, Susan

Cuningham, whispered boldly, "What a bum!" If she'd been caught it would have been the birch for her, too.

Facing that solid arse, I must confess I had seldom seen one in such prime condition for a rodding. Moreover, with the broad strap around the waist now secured, forcing the culprit to curve it up even more over the leathern boss beneath her pelvis there, the natural tremors of apprehension, unable to communicate themselves elsewhere in the body, sent their anxiety to the well parted cheeks. It was as if there were a seething beneath the skin there and, anxious to show her true mettle before her superiors, tall Miss Hall spent much time with her Prefect tensening the pose till the thick cheeks, which she prodded inspectingly, literally seemed to be bursting, the anal bud in full view.

"Mistress, do your duty," came Miss Temple's voice from the dais. "The first of four, if you please."

Miss Hall selected a dripping verge of the thicker kind, with more twigs than most. Her task was to lay the groundwork of the entire flogging and one invariably knew how bad this was to be by those first cuts. They should be "long," that is, whippily lapping round the right and forming a broad band of smart on which her successors could work as wished. The tips could send you half-crazed with pain when they bit in already livid skin.

The woman performed her assignment magisterially; it was an exemplary first dozen, really ferocious and perfectly timed.

She stood a pace or more back, measured off carefully, and cut like a tiger!

Zzzzzsch!

"Hah!"

"One," drawled the Prefect from the side.

The long sweeping stroke looked absolutely agonizing; it had driven up under the bum, making the round cheeks bound forwards and inscribing on them violet striations. The mistress had "taken" her target at just the right place; with spread legs she would have lost good tender flesh to have whipped any lower than she did—which was just above the intersection of the cheeks, or, as that ninny Susan Cuningham muttered to me, "Right behind the cunt."

Three more terrific cuts sliced into the same place, at good intervals. The girl took them in silence, her body jerking each time. She had not had a tenth of her count, yet her back could be seen sweating beneath the chandeliers, always burning even in daytime in this grim chamber.

Miss Hall's strength was astonishing us all. She whistled the wire-enwrapped twigs across the springy flesh, clawing up purple furrows. These were beginning to meld on the right into a single scalding contusion. After the ninth the girl gasped out "Oh God no!" but controlled herself. The dozen was completed with three brutal swipes that must have stung to the very soul. The girl let her upper body fall forward, gave a cry and straightened. While Miss Hall returned smiling to the dais, to receive the congratulations of our Headmistress, Neil bathed the sufferer's forehead and administered the smelling salts.

Miss Boyden was chosen to administer the next twelve, which could be given very slowly indeed. They were again merciless cuts, broadening the weal on the right and turning all on the left side the hue of the poppy and plum. Verily the girl was going to have

the skin flayed from her at this rate. She was groaning in agony and the salts were given again and again.

A large sigh swept the room after the third stripe of the third dozen had been given by Miss Emily Oakes, however. The blonde Latin mistress had taken a leaner verge, with perhaps only four long limbs bound in it. She could cut into the vividly tenderized meat now and did so, witheringly. After this stroke it was as if a razor had sliced: a ruby pearl swelled where a tail-end had fallen and Neil applied the stinging pimentade, painting into the graze. The girl was now in sorry state, for this burning solution, together with the rub of a bar of cattle salt that succeeded it, would now be driven fully in beneath the skin by succeeding cuts. And what cuts they were! The streaked rounds writhed ever more desperately, occasioning new tautening of the straps. Miss Oakes took three rods to her dozen, wanting the full penalty of tough tips to be felt, and by its end shards of wood were flying and the Duty Prefect's white-clad lap was marked by spicules of blood. At least two inches of skin on the right had been grazed away and the tips ate into wet stuff there, with unspeakable rigor. The girl shrieked at the last. And how the arse-cheeks now convulsed at the touch of the pimentade brush.

A sigh like low wind over wheat fields brushed the assembly then, as Scatcherd came down to give the *coup de grâce,* the last dozen, and she had been chosen too to apply the flail. With what diabolic skill did she cut. She did so "short," biting the tips into the full richness of weal in the right buttock-cheek. With what drear sound did they fall, each echoed by a shrill cry and a lurch that shook the very block. After each cut the buttocks spasmed as the girl gasped

speechlessly for air, her eyeballs bulging; she hung there in a trance, sweat pouring down her shoulder-blades, then relaxed like a lump, breathless—and Scatcherd sliced again.

"Mer-mer-meeeeeer-*ooooouigh!*"

The thick right cheek was no longer merely oozing its crimson dew, it was trickling in at least three places. Esteeming this welt benumbed, Miss Scatcherd then cut the left chub alone, finally "whipping in" so that the end of the tails nipped right inside the cheek, forming blood-clotted weals close to the anus.

When it was over, the girl was almost gone. She panted, making raw sounds, her head wrenched back to see what next her tormentress was preparing for her. Her brutalized buttocks seemed to throb, steaming.

"No more," she could be heard calling weakly, "no more, Ma'am, I do beseech you . . . in the name of God Whom you love, do not give me the cords. I am cut through entirely behind."

This babbling on the part of such a big girl frightened us exceedingly and had its effect on poor Jessica Cameron, trembling like a leaf and crying openly.

"You have sinned," said Miss Temple drily, "and must atone to the full. Ten strokes, Miss Scatcherd; let them be felt and take your time."

The martinet was another bitter, wicked instrument with which we were afflicted at Lowood. From a shiny wooden handle depended a number of hard cords given weight by soaking in water and rugosity by the tough knots made in them, the last of which were sometimes stiffened by sealing wax.

"For pity's sake . . . ooooh, mercy, mercy. . . ."

To receive these "master's" strokes the girl's legs

were brought together and extended behind her; a bar braced her knees absolutely straight and on the tumified cheeks, huddling and juddering together, the martinet ripped down. Its strokes are truly like red-hot tongs at the best of times, especially where the knots fall, and what they must have been like to the broad-arsed girl flayed in front of us that day I dread to think. All I know is, she howled. Miss Scatcherd whirled the thongs round her head to separate them and, rising a-tiptoe, brought them down with a thick matt sound into the martyrized flesh. After four they were wet and stained. Dark dots as big as peas were sewn across the full surface; with her last mighty swipes, given with all her power, the mistress was "lucky" enough to burst some of these blood-blisters which fairly spurted in complaint. When it was all over the girl was restored, stood up, and again lectured, after which she was led round the three ranks of the school as a lesson by the Prefect, her arms again behind her. She completed her calvary bowed over, hardly able to stand up, and making a continuous low groan. When she passed before us Minnies I had a full view of the arse which had been so cruelly cut into: it looked twice its size and blood runneled down the right thigh. I suspected it would be two weeks ere it was white again. Alas, each day of Solitary Confinement, on bread and water, was invariably accompanied by six of the best morning and night with a cane. Of Detention I shall recount the horrors to which we were there subjected below.

Useless to tell of Jessica Cameron's almost equal agony. During the flogging of her friend fear had made her "wee," as we used to say. A small pool was found between her feet, when she was called for; her

nose was rubbed in this and she was ordered another six. So altogether she suffered about as badly and her thin, ivory-skinned cheeks were fearfully raw by the time it was over. She too was paraded past us, sobbing.

When it was finished and we had filed out, there were, I regret to say, more bright glances exchanged, and hot hands held. The connoisseurs of the rod made their comments. All opined that Hall's first dozen was what had made the birching so "tight." One monster of thirteen avowed she had been able to come thrice, watching. I need say no more but that my own pulses were pounding, and my little slit wet.

As time passed, the seasons changed if the scene did not. With the passage of another year I was advanced into the Minor class, thanks in the main to my fine size and shape, and was allowed several keenly felt privileges, like rambles in the grounds unsupervised. Ever and always, of course, was I reminded by physical chastisement that I was a defective being, of an inferior race, whose superior I should strive to emulate—with stoicism, control, and courage. I had many faults and few redeeming points.

Never again did Miss Miller favor me as she had, and twice did she get me birched. The second occasion was worse, but the very worst of all such I ever had at Lowood was in my penultimate year when, in common with three other upper girls, I was involved in refractive behavior, bordering on rebellion, to our dormitory monitor. It was five dozen, a full sixty no less, after which the insulted prefect was permitted to take her revenge by placing twelve of the juiciest with a Duty cane on our quivering, virtually flayed undercheeks. It was hell itself, a long protracted pun-

ishment that took all the time from break to second Hall, for we swallowed our doses in turn, of a dozen each, and then the last two dozen together. The caning alone took a full three minutes and was one of the most agonizing I had ever had.

Moreover, we were not as usual allowed to go to the Recovery Room for the rest of the day, but had to dress and take our place in class and preparation for the remainder. We got permission to stand up for two whole days and our knickers had to be soaked off our flanks at the end of each. Our one recompense was the respect of our peers at sight of our ruined rears. To receive the cane on birched flesh is not an experience I wished to repeat and I was a mouse to the end of term. What's more, that fiend of a Prefect had given me much of my ration excessively low, even to the thighs.

Hitherto, therefore, I have recorded in detail and some chronological logic the events of my insignificant existence at Lowood. But I shall not conclude in the manner of a regular autobiography . . . I am only bound to invoke memory where I know her responses will possess some degree of interest, before I recount how I was taken on as a governess by Mr. Rochester, at Thornfield. A few lines only are necessary to help the reader to picture the connection, and my gradual growth to womanhood.

WHRRRPPP!

TEN!

"Yaowww!"

What a stroke. I screamed like a scalded cat, as the whippy ivory whacked into my wounded under-flesh. My buttocks bunched, spasming in swollen protest as the agony laved through them. Oh, Mr. Rochester was being strict tonight, very. My master's aim was sure. The tip was eating into wet meat now.

"Please please, sir," I babbled when my breath was back, "but spare me these last."

"Nonsense, Jane, they are going to do you the most good. So why would you want to miss them?"

The logic was ineluctable, since the law was his.

"Relax now," he said gently. "These are going to hurt."

10

I have not yet alluded to the visits to Lowood of Mr. Brocklehurst. They occurred at the end of each term and occasionally during them. His absence, usually with his friend the archdeacon, was a relief to us. I need not say how we dreaded these inspective comings. His presence invariably inspired perfect dread, and we were aware of it by some schoolgirl sixth sense. Like the Lord of Hosts he came to chasten, and chastened.

One morning after his carriage had deposited him and we were in class, that familiar long stride measuring the passage announced his round of inspection. I was under Miss Scatcherd and sat terrified as the cortege approached.

It was an impressive one and we rose like soldiers as it entered the schoolroom. First strode in Mr. Brocklehurst himself, doubling an endless cane under his chin; behind him was Miss Temple, smiling as ever, clad in stone-hued trousers of velvet, fitting very tight, and a brief black velvet gilet which revealed rather than concealed; behind her, in turn, also in short dark velvet tunic and pin-clean tucker was the Duty mar'm of the day, red-headed Miss Boyden, carrying an instrument. There was a Duty Prefect all in white, Matron Harden creaking on her crutches and two maids in attendance, with buckets that boded badly.

"Sit down, sit down," he said, acknowledging Miss Scatcherd's smiling curtsey. He it was who was about the only person that harpy ever smiled at.

I sat looking straight in front of me, without a breath, hoping the air would somehow make me invisible. I had not seen the Reverend since Gateshead and he looked twice as dark and impressive today.

Brows beetling he surveyed us from the dais for a long time in silence, doubling that appalling cane. Our hearts were pounding like pistons as he began to speak:

"You young ladies are aware, I believe, that you are not here to be accustomed to habits of luxury and indulgence, but to be rendered wholly hardy, patient, self-denying. I take this opportunity of reminding you of the sufferings of the primitive Christians, of the

torments of the martyrs; of the exhortations of our blessed Lord himself, calling upon his disciples to take up their cross and follow Him, of His divine consolations, 'if ye suffer hunger or thirst for my sake, happy are ye.' "

The man began to walk through our quaking rows. I was in a more forward one and breathed a sigh as he passed behind, beyond my ken. The silence was becoming suffocating. We heard him pause by a desk.

"You—what is your name?"

"Black, Mona, sir."

"Have you been thrashed this week?"

"Yes, sir," piped the voice.

"Hurt?"

"Yes, sir."

"How many?"

"Six, sir. Failing in Recitation."

"Do you good?"

"Yes, sir."

"Hm. Very well. Since it was so salutory you shall have the same again tonight. Inscribe this girl for six and, Duty Mistress, see that you work her tight and low. Make her wish she had a smaller pair of buttocks."

"I shall, sir, with pleasure," said Miss Boyden from the side.

The brute paced on. Again he stopped.

"Name?"

"Marowney, Audrey, sir."

"You're idle, aren't you?"

"I try not to be, sir."

"Nonsense, I can see it in your eyes. Put this child down for a fellow six for Contradicting. Now then,

Audrey Marowney, let's see how you fancy a taste of my cane across the top of those tightly stretched knickers of yours. A nice fleshy thing. Come, bend right over your desk and put it up for me now. Skirt up. Good, so. Let's see how you cut, from above."

There was a deathly still, then the cane made its whirry *whupp!*

The girl gave a harsh gasp. The mistresses looked on smiling. Another meaty thump broke the silence. I blinked and jumped. The air positively resounded to the third.

"Hooooo!" Her feet could be heard trampling in the stocks.

"Feeling warmer, Miss Marowney?" He delivered the fourth, solid cut and I do not think there was a drop of blood in any of our faces in that class. "You a Major, child?"

"Nunno, sir, Minor."

"Well you have a major pair of posteriors and I'll give you another."

"Oh sir, nosssir . . . OWWW!"

"There. Now sit down on those fat idle cheeks, keep your hands in your lap and your backbone straight. I believe you have some good marks there to work on, Duty mistress."

Miss Boyden grinned. "Six of the best in my room at four o'clock, Audrey."

"Yer-yess, Miss."

"This girl here,"—and I heard Mr. Brocklehurst's cane tapping a new desk—"see that she gets two hours Detention this afternoon for Slouching."

"Yes, sir," said the Duty Prefect, inscribing.

"Make sure she spends a half hour of it on the stoutest carrot you've got. Right up her."

"It shall be done," said Miss Boyden, still with her impish grin.

There was then a long and positively electric silence. Only the creak of leather boots was heard and then suddenly a panicky whimper shivered our spines. It came from the back of the room.

"Oh no, sir, please, sir . . . not me, sir, please oh please spare me oh no sir, please sir. . . ."

And so on.

"If there's one thing I can't stand it's a *sniveling* girl."

"No sir, please sir. . . ."

The poor child appeared to have completely broken down. We sat horrified, spine-chilled while the sound of a physical struggle ensued, the girl pleading and whimpering the while. Finally Mr. Brocklehurst said, "Get her over for me, tight," and the monitor hurried forward.

Thhhh-whack!

"Yah!"

Two . . . three . . . four, each followed by a cry.

"Hold her still."

"I'm sorry, sir, she's struggling so."

"Get her tight for this last one or you'll feel twelve like this across your own backside, Prefect."

THHHHWLACK!

"Yeow!"

A pause. The Reverend's breathing could be heard, alongside the sinner's weeping whimpers.

"A thoroughly disgraceful exhibition. Miss Temple, I am sending this child up to you for the birch."

"With pleasure," said our noble Head, in her soft purr of a voice. "Three dozen on Saturday. For re-

sisting chastisement."

The man came slowly forward. Every mind in that class wanted but one thing—his immediate absence. He stood facing Miss Satcherd for a long while. When he broke the silence every heart dropped a yard. Mine fell to the region of my heels like a ton of bricks.

"I mean to make an example. Which of these girls needs whipping, Miss S.?"

The mistress replied quietly, "They all do, sir, at varying times."

Mr. Brocklehurst nodded in agreement, bending his silky stick under his chin. "You are right. It is what they understand. I've a mind to order a whipping for every pair of cheeks in this room. Do you remember when I once flogged the whole school at a time, Miss Temple?"

"Vividly, sir," breathed that woman.

"Went through 'em like a dose of salts, didn't we? And I'll wager the last one felt fully as tight as the first."

"They didn't seem to like it one whit."

"Well—which is the laziest in this room?"

Miss Satcherd gave the closest to a sly smile I had ever seen on her lips. After a moment she said, "Helen Burns."

"Burns! Burns . . . stand out, Burns."

There was a soft movement behind me, accompanied by a stifled sigh, and Helen slipped from her desk and up the aisle, her short skirt swinging over her full posteriors. She stood facing Mr. Brocklehurst, almost as tall as he in her heels, her back to us, quivering, doomed.

"You Helen Burns?"

"Yes, sir."

"What have you to say for yourself?"

"Nothing, sir."

The man smiled. "Good. This is good." He walked round her and, raising the skirt behind, ran an assessing hand over the long and opulent slopes of Helen's superb buttocks. "You're lazy, aren't you?"

"Yes, sir," she admitted meekly.

"I know a lazy rump when I see one." Then he tipped her sweet round chin in his fingers and his pale eyes bore into her brimming mauve orbs. "Not been thrashed today?"

"No, sir."

"Ye're going to be now." Still gazing into the girl's eyes, he said, "Do we have a soko, Miss Boyden?"

"We do, sir," agreed the Duty mistress with alacrity. My eyes flicked to the side but one of the maids was obscuring my vision there.

"Ever had the soko, girl?"

"No, sir."

"I think you'll agree it's twice as tight nor an ordinary birch, after a few. Take 'em off."

Impassively, her lovely face as gentle as ever, Helen began the unbuttoning necessary for removal of her knickers. Miss Boyden came forward whistling the dreaded soko through the air and saying, "This should make her sit up a bit, I think."

Our mentor took the rod and tested it, desolatingly, on the air himself. The soko birch was the worst instrument we were subjected to at Lowood. I felt sick looking at it, then. It was composed of long lean strips of greyish-white whalebone, used in stiffening corsets; at Lowood three of these were set, in parallel spacing, in a sort of wooden handle which

thus held them half an inch apart, so that one might not diminish another's smart. It was simply that these fiendish fangs were, as well as whippy, so intolerably tough. The tips were hard as stone and as Mr. Brocklehurst thrashed them on the tabletop now they made wiry raps that took all taste from our drying mouths. They were far too cruel for schoolgirls to bear, the weals lasted weeks, yet they were an approved article of furniture in even the most elegant ladies academies. Helen Burns looked on apprehensively as the Prefect in waiting attended to the man's laconic order, "Bare those buttocks now." She was to be made into an "example" for the second time that term. When the monitor had finished tucking her skirt up in her belt, Helen turned modestly a little, presenting her back alone to Mr. Brocklehurst.

The latter extended the quivery rod to Miss Boyden with a smirking bow.

"Your honor, mistress. D'ye think ye can draw with a dozen?"

"I'll do my best, sir."

Miss Satcherd interposed. "If I might be so bold, Reverend. This is a hardened, cynical child. She can take a thorough count."

"Very well, make it fifteen."

Helen looked sickly at the soko. Her lips had fallen open. She turned yet more, very slowly. I began to feel a heat behind my face. There was a girl across the aisle from me, moving on her seat in a rhythmic, surreptitious way. Suddenly we knew we were all aware of the strong penile tube that had grown perpendicular up one side of Mr. Brocklehurst's thin fawn trousers. Fatty quiverings shook Helen's hams.

"How do'ye want her, Ma'am? Bent?"

"Slightly bent, sir, if you please."

"Backboard," the ogre then snapped, "straps!"

The Prefect hurried forward. Helen was facing fully away from us now, superbly bared. Her arms were hoist in the backboard and then, as if fettering some desperate fugitive, the monitor now applied a series of straps to her lower limbs—at ankle, knee, and thigh.

"Good," said the reverend when this was done, "now call on your courage, girl, and think of your Saviour. Matron, fig her." Mrs. Harden creaked elaborately forward. When the vile ginger suppository had been duly inserted, against clenching, Mr. Brocklehurst rapped his cane on the class mistress's table. "Take up your position, girl, and prepare to suffer."

With a last lost look at him Helen realized she had no other course than to hop forward in her bonds. She did so, attained the table and leant across it. She was simply secured there by the medium of the maids, one at either end of her backboard. Her superb crupper spread, deeply divided, her thonged legs a trifle bent beneath as the upper body held to the worn deal tabletop. I began to feel giddy. The anal crater gleamed slickly central.

"Now flog her, Miss, as you have never flogged before." With arrogant contempt for feminine feelings the man then stroked up his monstrous erection, which had brought a blush to many a watching face, and throughout the chastisement he often left his hand there, or stroked appreciately, the while he gave instructions for the greater severity.

Then the silence stiffened. Miss Boyden drew back.

She swung and cut—the whirring whoosh was twice as high in pitch as that of the wooden birch.

Whu-whu-whuwhillllck!

Three frightful dark furrows were clawed across the arse. Helen jerked, then the inner cheeks could be seen cringing as the true pain chewed into them. She had had one.

"Well cut," said the Reverend. "But come down more, Ma'am, and you will draw quicker."

She did. She "drew" at five, a frightful slice that made poor Helen shoot her legs back. Six, seven, eight. . . . She now had two dozen thin black weals, several bleeding, across her rump; yet she had not uttered a sound. This did not please Mr. Brocklehurst.

"Does it hurt you, girl?"

Forced to speak, Helen suddenly yelled—"Yes, sir! I am in hell."

"In order to prepare you for heaven. Whip on, mistress, and see if you can make this stubborn sinner sing."

A frightful beauty fell. The whalebone tips lashed inexorably into the so vulnerable fat and Helen cried and bent her knees. She caught another whistler just like that and I became aware that the girl across the aistle, who had clearly been frotting herself against the little saddle-like riser in our seats, which made us part our hinds, had stiffened suddenly, tense. I saw her face. It was dazed with rapture, lost.

"Good. A fine cut. Splendid."

Some of the welts now exuded blood all along them. Helen was being cut to ribbons. When it was all over she fell back and thumped hard to the floor before us, still in her backboard. She writhed there

like a worm, mewing her agony, and grinding her bottom into the floorboards. But when she looked up at our patron it was with tears in her eyes, tears of gratitude—"Th-thank you, sir." She bent awkwardly and kissed his soil-stained boots.

"Take this girl up to the infirmary," said Mr. Brocklehurst coldly, "and have her attended to. *That* is how you all should be punished. And daily."

With which he left the room, followed by his grim cortege. When they had gone, breathless silence held the room. Glossy, gleaming, Miss Satcherd stared at us from her dais, head back, triumphant also. She was clearly very excited. The hands which held the cane across her thighs trembled, and her breasts showed her hastened breathing.

She came slowly down among us lesser mortals, her lean legs swinging. Every single one of us was terrified. Chastisement roamed the room like a beast. She advanced slowly, smiling in a strange fixed way. Finally, she stopped and faced the girl across from me who had been masturbating during the sorry seance.

"Stand up, Barbara Tennant," she said. She had seen. The girl rose, knowing. She began to whimper. The mistress felt between her legs. She said nothing for a moment, still rigidly smiling, like some puppet. Then in a whisper she got out, as someone suffocated, "Report to me at six o'clock. And God help you until a quarter after."

It had to be admitted, however, that The Brock (as we used between ourselves to refer to him) was eminently just. It was during my penultimate year that I had chief occasion to attest to this. By this time I had in common with my colleagues grown

wholly to appreciate the finer niceties of the rod, and even to enjoy its play upon the temptingly denuded backside of a lesser girl.

During one of his longer stays, of inspection and diversion, the Reverend caught out a culprit well fitted for his mettle. This was a butcher's boy, a big sullen lout who used to deliver his goods to the kitchens on certain mornings of the week. This ignoble lad had contrived to find a grating through which he could peep up into a place where we senior girls were permitted to repair to relieve ourselves. So our natural needs had afforded him many a moment of masturbatory solace. Caught in *flagrante delicto,* with a prick as stiff as some crowbar, the spunky boy had been sentenced instantly to a severe whipping by Mr. Brocklehurst.

I was one of the three innocent girls whom he was at the time over-, or to put it bluntly, under-seeing. When Miss Temple summoned us and told us that we would be witness to the punishment of this rash butcher's boy, there was much natural merriment amongst us. The whipping was to take place in a small stone dairy shed apart from the main house, and we three went to it a-twitter of excitement. We wanted to see this dolt who had taken advantage of us behind, as it were, well whipped.

He was. A whipping-scale had been set up in the small dairy and we three lined ourselves on a step one side of it, with a grandstand view. The place was bare but for a can or two, and some curd. Presently there was a hubbub outside and the big boy was brought in at the double, already whimpering and pleading, his hands fettered in front of him. He had on only his shirt and boots and he was led in like a

great clattering dray-horse by leather-caped Neil, clearly enjoying her work. Mr. Brocklehurst brought up the rear, in shirt-sleeves, carrying the veritable rapier of a long, lean riding-whip.

The lad did not look at us but whimpered all the time, "Please sir, oh please sir," the while Neil deftly drew him a-tiptoe by his wrists cuffed to the whipping-scale. She knotted his shirt-ends over one shoulder and the muscular bottom was superbly nude. There was still a strong curve in his thing in front, at which we girls nudged each other gigglingly.

"Well, lad, not in the sullens today?" said the Reverend gloatingly, pushing his own shirtsleeve higher over the Dutch cheese of a bicep. "Let's see if ye still feel randy after a few of these."

The boy hung limp, awaiting. Whether it was the presence of the fair sex to his nakedness or not, his thing curved even stiffer, like a stallion's, but at the first unfeeling cuts it subsided.

Mr. Brocklehurst truly knew how to flog a bum in *style*. The soft whistle of his switch ended with a sound that made us flinch. He twined the waxy whipcord excruciatingly about the full thick arse, like some expert swordsman—and the contest was unequal. The buttocks soon began to make nervous bounds, the skin shuddered as the lashes licked in, leaving crimson traces fast turning blue. The cord cut like fury. What a whipping!

We three devoured it with unashamed greed, I fear, admiring our mentor with a kind of dumb rapture. The boy began to howl, and dance, reeling on the whip-scale, until he purely screamed. I counted to twenty from that cunning wrist but still the Reverend was unslaked exempting no cranny of skin till

the entire buttock was bleeding and raw. The floor was speckled with blood.

"There, my lad, let that teach you to look up ladies' skirts. That make you want to wank off, do it?"

The butcher's boy hung exhausted. At some prearranged signal between herself and the good Reverend, Neil now advanced with a smile. To our astonishment she gently palmed the now retired penis in her soft gloved hand. It responded at once and, fisting it expertly, she quickly made it grow, grinning the while.

The boy began to groan, and trample on his toes. The stiff cock kicked blood-heavy. Mr. Brocklehurst flicked him hard with the whip-tip, on the left. Then another stinger on the right, where the flesh was fairly raw. The boy began his St. Vitus' dance again, moaning and groaning with his pleasure-pain as Neil continued to wank him. The whipping picked up, and so did his cock! Relinquishing it, Neil let it stand out turgid, bobbing, from his belly. Then with a quick nod to the Reverend she grasped the ball-sack and started milking it. Concomitantly the thrasher applied his whip with a zestful will and the boy wailed at the top of his lungs, "YAAAA-OIHHHH!"

Together they forced the ejaculation from him. The engorged cockhead furiously spat, jetting in cloudy gouts that arched two yards or more, falling audibly on the stone dairy floor. Fisting the balls most painfully, Neil caused her human hose to spout like a geyser, throbbing up its clots of semen which went flying through the air the while Mr. Brocklehurst belabored the agonized posterior with all his might. When it was over the boy hung panting,

speechless, slack, and Mr. Brocklehurst himself was sweating.

"*That* will teach him to look up your bottoms, I think," he opined to us then. "If you wish to apply extra cuts, you are at liberty to do so."

We declined the offer, curtseyed and returned to the main buildings with lowered heads, thoughtfully.

But the worst I ever saw during my terms at Lowood was the birching of Julie Severn and her friend, both of whom got the full six dozen that was allegedly our maximum at the block. They had been found guilty of a strange crime.

Julie was a monitor and her comrade, whose name eludes me, almost so. Now it was known that Miss Temple corporeally chastised her own mistresses, notably the under ones, at intervals for faults; such corrections were carried out in the utmost secrecy, at night, and there were maids on guard throughout the corridors to see that no girl ever witnessed the offender stumbling back to her quarters, after.

For these floggings were evidently atrociously severe, on the principle that a mistress should be able to suffer what she prescribed. Julie Severn had somehow learnt that one was impending; there was a trapdoor above the bathing section of her dorm and on the night concerned she and her tribadic friend hoisted themselves through it, walked the rafters until they found themselves full over the Chastisement Chamber where the penance was taking place—and they watched it through a crack.

Amazingly enough, Mrs. Harden had been suffering. Yes, neither her age nor her stump sufficed to spare the cruel Matron who was hoist over a horse, her yard of crupper the color of uncooked beef as a

gardener of the grounds applied the martinet to it before the Head and her assembled mistresses. It was a grim sight indeed, so the girls later said, yet strangely exciting to see the stump of leg kick out sideways at each cut.

So absorbed had they then become in their mutual frigging that they had made a noise, been caught, and hauled off to Solitary. Sent for, Mr. Brocklehurst convened the school. Never shall I forget the fear he inspired in his seat of honor at the top of our Long Chamber as the two culprits, who had given up all hope, were brought in naked, their arms bound behind them. He walked calmly down and scrutinized them closely for some full five minutes. Finally, he went behind and examined them minutely, finishing with each girl's lovely long brown hair. Behind these living medals his words fell like the knell of doom—"These two top-knots must be cut off."

Miss Temple seemed to remonstrate.

"Madam," he pursued, "I have a Master to serve whose kingdom is not of this world; my mission is to mortify in these girls the lusts of the flesh. I repeat, their hair must first be cut off. . . ."

It was. And their heads were shaved. Each had to be curried—that is, a curry comb used for the coat of horses drawn up their buttocks till they bled—and then each swallowed the awful medicine of six full dozen with the soko, venomously applied by avenging mistresses. Suffice it to say that by the last two dozen the tails fell on wet flesh and neither girl had voice to scream. They had to be assisted in their calvary around the room after it was over. Both were reduced to the Minimus rank for the rest of term, with numerous other additive punishments to match.

But there were other reasons why Mr. Brocklehurst came to Lowood than mere inspection, and correction. And to these I propose to append a chapter here.

WHHHHRPP!

The eleventh cut streaked across my already deeply bruised under-rump, the ivory tip making my right cheek literally jump.

I shrieked aloud.

I WAS IN HELL FIRE ITSELF!

Impossible to describe my contortions upon the triangle then. I fairly made it creak. Sweat streamed cold from my forehead and hot down my back. Great merciful God in heaven, Lord of Hosts give me the last cut soon . . . soon . . . and have it done with forever.

11

Until this point I have refrained from allaying my reader's natural curiosity concerning what sexual instruction, if any, we girls received at Lowood. It was, like everything else there, thorough and brutal. I shall come to it, covering what went on during my own incumbency within those grim walls.

Every girl at Lowood was personally deflowered by the Reverend Brocklehurst. This was his *droit du seigneur,* and his mark of mastery upon us. It generally happened at some point in one's first, or Minimus, year but was unannounced. Whenever the carriage wheels of his brougham grated on the gravel, and we knew he had come for one of his stays, we

junior girls trembled. We could be sent for at any time, for the stake of that so solid manhood to be driven through us.

This state of trepidation was carefully increased by the concupiscent great girls who loved to tease us about the event, incidentally exciting themselves. For though as painful as possible the defloration was evidently intensely arousing and there were few of them who would not have given much to feel that gristly tree-trunk in their guts again; there was the story of one girl who so dwelt on it in her imagination she could barely think of aught else, and wrought herself up to a pitch of pure crazed ecstasy. One day, it was said, hearing Mr. Brocklehurst's tread upon a landing, she wildly threw herself at his feet, embracing and licking at his boots, imploring him to take her, then and there. The man had apparently given her a ferocious flogging with his cane and then buggered her, leaving her in an almost insensible state of tormented frustration. Throughout the rest of that term the poor thing had stubbornly continued to masturbate at the memory, despite repeated birchings when found.

"You're going to feel it up to here," said a great girl to me once, in a grinning group. And she touched the top of my head. "Right to the back of your skull."

"And if you're tight, Eyre, I swear it'll come boiling out of your ears," said another. "Just see if it don't. That man pumps pints."

"It feels like a garden hose gone off inside you."

"Too bad if you've got a tough membrane, Jane; he'll split you like a fruit."

"You'll feel it for a week after."

"Bam!" A tall girl, smiling broadly, beat a fist into

one palm. "I felt as if he'd bust open my whole belly."

"He split me so wide I thought I was going to shit out his stuff when he came."

"Oooooh, what wouldn't I give for that sausage up me now!"

This indecent raillery may seem harmless enough, but poor Joan Walker, whose narrow loins looked as if they would be broken in two by any such rogering, it reduced to tears.

I trembled. "Der-does he flog you first?"

"Yes," said one. And then, as if at a signal, the great girls all turned and went off together, arm in arm down the corridor, in pace, their tiny skirts whisking over their important thin white knickers, through which their buttocks bloomed. It was with a curious admixture of terrified trepidation and unconscious yearning that we awaited the inevitable rape by the Reverend; and when mousy Estella Moore suffered first of us four new-knicks that year, I know I for one was deeply jealous. The girl was sly and smilingly evasive to our questions for a whole week after; indeed, she looked contented as a cat after cream. She was a big girl, able to support a battering, I suppose, and he had allegedly done it in her thrice. Sometimes he took on two or more in a night, but we were all done separately. My turn came at the end of my first year at Lowood and it was a complete surprise; I had not known the man was present at all.

I awoke in the dead of night to find a black-gloved hand over my mouth. A figure was standing beside my bed, holding a lamp. It was Neil, smelling strongly of her stiff kid outfit. She gestured to keep silent, then whispered, "Follow me."

The whole dormitory was darkened and asleep as

I slipped out of bed and followed the lamp held aloft by Neil and richly shining on her opulent nether contours. I had on only my nightgown and was bare of foot. Tousled and sleepy I followed the majestic figure down stairs, up others, along passages in silence. All was dark and ominous and I scarce knew where I was until we abutted abruptly at an all too familiar carved door—Miss Temple's. Suddenly I caught my breath.

Neil looked at me, smiling. "When you leave this room, Jane, you will be a woman," she said gravely.

My legs melted. "Oooh, Neil . . . I'm so frightened . . . is he . . . ?"

Seeing I would not knock, she did so for me and opened the door at the gruff growl from within. All too soon it had closed behind me. I felt sick with fear at what I saw.

The great chamber was little lit. A large log fire comfortably flamed and there was an oil lamp on the long leathern desk top, throwing its mellow glow over two figures, Miss Temple and the Reverend Brocklehurst. I caught my breath for it was with a little thrill almost of desecration that I saw our Headmistress naked from the waistband of her taut blue velvet trousers up. She was lounging on one arm of Mr. Brocklehurst's chair and I felt naughty looking at her so and dropped my eyes. She had adorable titties, small chubby apples with little aureole but ink-dark nipples.

Her glasses winked reassuringly and she smiled as she beckoned me to come forward in front of them. I went to the desk.

Mr. Brocklehurst's face was swarthy and shadowed, but he too was laughing and had I not feared

him so, I should have called him handsome. He reclined against the tall rest, wearing only a flounced shirt of the finest lawn which, I could see, was opened to the waist, exposing his muscular and darkly hairy chest.

"The lamb to the slaughter," he chuckled gently. I trembled like an aspen. It was happening, finally it was happening at last, and there was no way in the world I could stop it. Something deep within me thrilled like a bow-string as he picked up his great long cane from the desk-top. They had both been drinking from cut-glass carafes, Miss Temple's golden and the man's port-red.

"Come, Jane," said Miss Temple in a voice I had never heard her use before, so soft and dewy with smiling sensuality was it, "do not be so frightened."

"Know what you are here for, girl?"

"Yer-yess, sir."

"What?"

"To take . . . for you to take my maidenhood."

He grinned largely. "D'ye think I can?"

"Yes, sir."

"Come, let's see it then. Come, come," as I hesitated and his stick twitched at my nightgown, "your honey-pot, child. Let's get a good look at it now."

I raised the hem of my gown to my waist. I had by this time quite grown out and was inordinately proud of what I then showed, just above the desk, on the sill of my thighs. My bush was black and thick and the lips it hid were fat and ripe. I had a bulgy mons, "prime for skewering," as more than one girl had remarked in the dormitory. Well, now it was going to get it.

"Strip altogether."

Mr. Brocklehurst stared long and intently at the plum. "That's what I'd call a soulful twat, wouldn't you, Hilda, heh, heh?" As he spoke I heard something knock beneath the desk, his side. I gulped, petrified. "Nice tough hymen, heh. Matron says you have a good one. Not too much horseback stuff in your youth. Mm, wet and sensuous. Yes, yes."

As he spoke he had been prodding me knowingly, first the juicy sentinel which felt surprisingly stiff, then inside my vulva, the bendy tip coming up against my inner membrane which it tested as on a thumb. Finally, he extracted the end of the rod, sniffed it appreciately and took a swig of port.

"Heavens, you're going to feel this, girl. Taut as a drum and far more springy. You'll never forget it all your life."

"Also, you'll never regret it all your life," said Miss Temple, standing up and stretching superbly. "Mr. Brocklehurst is doing you a great honor, Jane. There aren't many men built like him and on your wedding night you'll be glad he served you. So will your husband. He'll open you right up, just you see. But first come over here and we'll do some exercises to help you take him."

She led me gently to a large rug in front of the fire. Here I had to do a succession of energetic exercises —squat bends, toe-touchings, then hopping in the squat position, then on my back with legs over the head, parted widely, stretching, stretching. Finally, panting and wet with sweat, I lay back to see Miss Temple in the mists above me, smiling serenely as ever and I couldn't help wondering if she had felt the bludgeon up that trim velvet belly of hers. She guessed my thoughts with a chuckle.

"Of course every woman loves to feel thoroughly filled and replete, Jane. He'll give it me later and I shall be grateful to you for taming him down a little, first. There are times when he makes me feel almost too impaled." It scarcely seemed possible I was speaking to Miss Temple when I said, "Can we get it over soon, Ma'am, please?"

"Yes, but first I shall have to whip you a bit," she went on in the same kindly tone. "Nothing too terrible, just to make you all nice and tingly."

She chose a long, withy birch and made me bend forward with hands on my knees, feet apart. Oooh! how they stung! What vinegary cuts! I do not know how many she gave me, laughing all the while, but I soon shrieked up at their intensity, hopping and clasping. And in that state I was led back to the man, yes like a lamb to the slaughter.

"Now I'll give you a few on the back."

These too stung appallingly and left me doubled, gasping, clutching my armpits.

"God, Hilda, I tell you I feel so hard my teeth ache. I've absolutely got to have her now."

He stood up and I slowly raised my eyes. Only to feel I had been struck in the face.

The lawn shirt ended at his thighs. It was wide parted all down and from the furry ball-sack at his center reared the most manly masthood I had ever imagined. It was prodigious, a belly-high erection, dark and bobbing as he . . . *it* . . . came towards me. I recoiled, hand to mouth.

"Oh sir . . . oh please oh please, sir," I quavered like a ninny.

"Think this little dipper can plumb y'r smudge pot, Jane Eyre?"

The erection was on me. The fat tube was darker than I had seen, heavy with blood, while the great slab of meat that was the cockhead, with its thick corona, seemed to be palpitating to get at, into me. The sliced eye, whitely oozing, accused my very essense. The entire organ had the rigidity of throbbing iron and to think I was to be "done," hewn in half by . . . I turned to run.

Miss Temple caught me by an earlobe and swung me back before I had gone a pace.

"Isn't it a beauty, Jane?" she hissed hotly. "It spits like a clyster when he comes. Here."

She led me to a small low back less ottoman. I fell back on it, legs sprawled either side, head half-conscious. The good woman advised me to grip the little polished wood bar at that end, in order to withstand the siege. She herself straddled there, holding my shoulders. Suddenly I looked up, and squeaked.

He still had the shirt on, but no more. His strong black-haired thighs were either side the ottoman, his monstrous member rampant between them. In the firelight the great barrel seemed to have grown, I should never get a half of it up me. . . .

"Oh sir . . . sir!"

A glass clattered at my teeth. Miss Temple poured brandy down my throat.

"Feel game, girl?" he asked in a gruff though at the same time gentle tone. I nodded bleakly. I could not take my eyes off that . . . thing.

"I'll, I'll do my best, sir."

I heard him mutter something to Miss Temple. They were astride me at either end and then I saw him reach up and fondle her elastic titties. His prick gave a savage, mule-like kick. This index of its

strength drained the last of mine from me and when his hands lifted me under the buttocks I was unresisting, listless. I did not remain so for long.

Like a huge slug the furiously empurpled kidney of the head slipped in my parted lips. It felt heavy, loaded, and, gritting my teeth, I shut my eyes. Then gradually, kneading my bottom halves in his powerful hands, he nosed in and out of the top of my vulva, caressing my clitoris with his Cyclops eye. I came rapidly to life, blinked open my eyes—"Oh sir, what are you . . . oh dear God, sir. . . !"

They were bent forward and kissing above me as with a strangled gasp I gave a short squirting spasm round his cockhead. He laughed.

"I do believe the little mischief has come!"

"Give it her now, Broughton, right through and up her throat!"

They were talking in undertones but I had closed my eyes again, for it was coming in earnest. He had plugged me with his glib tube yet further and I felt as if I could barely breathe. Nothing existed. Nothing but the rhythmic probing as his head felt out the strength of my membrane. He splayed open my buttocks further and I uncontrolledly gasped out, "Do it . . . give it to me, sir . . . ah get it done!"

He slid out—the length of that gristle!—and I heard him saying something to Miss Temple. There was a pause while my whole hips were held on the top of his meatus, and then the world went mad.

"YEOAIEEEEEEEE!"

The room rang to my unearthly scream. It must have been heard throughout that holy edifice. In perfect concert Mr. Brocklehurst and Miss Temple made me skewer myself on that stake. The former

squeezed between finger and thumb two morsels of buttock flesh most wounded by the whip while the latter pinched my nipples with unspeakable acerbity. I lunged upwards, shrieking, at which moment the man split my fig and plunged his full length into me in one.

I was dismembered. It felt as if a fist had slammed up my entire being. The head ended under my ribs. I fought for breath, found none, tried to kick but could not.

"Good," said the Reverend, "now let's fuck the little devil in earnest."

By the time I got hold of myself I realized I was doubled back like a ball, my thighs held tight on my chest by firm Miss Temple as well as my ravisher . . . and I could but thresh a foot or two for movement. Dear Heaven alive! My face seemed but inches off my vulva, affording me a loge-like view of my present impalement as the great greasy, blood-flecked member now drove down into my guts almost vertically. Squeezed down, I was no more than a simple sleeve for penis.

"Oh sir, sir . . . mercy!"

"Well, Jane, which rod d'ye like best?"

His bloodshot face was miles above me as he pounded on with his merciless skewering. I was sheer cunt. And suddenly I knew I was coming as I never had before. I was slick with sweat and a steam rose before my eyes but I remember I said in a steady tone, "Sir, if you wish to . . . know . . . I think I am going to spend. . . ."

"I know you are," he grunted, snorting. He joggled me for a second, then rammed hard home.

"UINGH!"

I was stuffed to the gills, my eyeballs bursting, but suddenly my whole lower body clamped to his rock-hard cock. I felt myself streaming down its sides in unending ecstasy for what seemed like minutes, and then I lay back limp, gasping like any stranded fish.

High above me as well as in me the man drained port like water as Miss Temple handed him the restorative glass. He had not come. He was as hard as ever. My legs now hung limply astride the towel Miss Temple had evidently placed beneath my bottom, and Mr. Brocklehurst started work in earnest. Holding my pelvis high by the peach-halves he commenced a steady, reaming ramming, screwing the slick sausage deep into me, gouging and nuzzling the back of my womb.

"Oh God, sir, come," I begged in desperation, with tears in my eyes. "Spurt into me, sir, I do beg you. You have split me in two, now for God's sake spare me and go off."

He laughed, the while. Finally, after an eternity of thudding, he seemed to grunt, and swell.

"Isn't it lovely, Jane?" The Headmistress bent over me, fondling one of my titties.

"But I'm ger-going to," I bleated in sweet misery, "I'm going to come uggh. . . ."

She grinned and tweaked me.

"Jove, she fucks like butter!"

I wailed as it began. High above, it seemed, I saw two writhing insects, my plump legs, entwine themselves of their own volition round the thrusting waist and I buckled sickly upwards, stabbing myself on his colossal member, squirting in spurts. What bliss!

"The little mischief is coming all the time."

"It must have been that birching did it."

The lubricant of my love juices eased his entry and allowed him to penetrate and pummel more deeply within me. I was drained of all energy by the ecstasy and simply hung like a rag dog, legs lolling, my hips held glued to his by his hands beneath my buttocks.

The brute did not stop for a second. He was now slucking his bloody cylinder into me with driving force that took all breath from me. Our groins met with wet bruising thuds. I was being properly "done." My head hanging back on the ottoman I lay with lifeless arms and was fucked to the core and oh! beyond. I was a sheer sleeve of sex. Would the man never finish?

Looking up glassily I could see Miss Temple's bunched buttocks, in their pale blue velveteen breeches, as she straddled over me. She was avidly pressing two fingers into the lozenge of her central self and I thought bitterly, through gritted teeth, How would you like to be rammed like this, Ma'am?

"Lord, Broughton, but you are rogering her soundly."

He panted hoarsely, "Could fuck this twat all night . . . but get in better other way . . . the cervical slant. . . ." He was pulling my behind halves so apart by now that each of his rammings was echoed by a short, startled fart. All at once he slid out and the engorged monster, sticky with my gluttonous glue as well as blood, reared hotly before me. It had not had enough.

"Come, Jane," the mistress coaxed. She sat me up, half-dazed as I was, and poured more scalding brandy down my throat. It instantly revived me and I looked down at the thick cream, streaked with red,

that leaked to the towel between my legs. Ravished was the word.

"Well, Jane Eyre," the man mocked as I rose unsteadily, "did you feel something, after all?"

"Yes, sir."

"Come, you're a passionate child and we've only just begun. I'm going to take ye dog wise, from the back, now that I've opened you up a bit and I wager you'll feel it twice as deep."

"Oh please, sir," I begged hectically, "please shoot off into me."

"I'll shoot off," he said grimly, "and when I do, you'll feel it clear behind your eyeballs."

I was bent close over the desk with my legs apart. Miss Temple stationed herself at my head and held my hands, pulling me forward. I quivered like a willow as I felt the wet turgid piston in between my ass cheeks. I looked down and back. The fat head nosed between my swollen lips and then suddenly the whole limb sluiced into me like a sword.

"UINKK!"

I gaped up with disbelievingly dismay into the mistress' smiling face. This time he jammed me to the chest, I'd have sworn.

"It's toooo . . . big . . . uingh! Ooooh. . . . Uingh! . . . UINGH!"

My thighs vised to the desk edge by his own, the monster had me impaled like a butterfly on a page. Grunting rhythmically he stuffed and crammed every inch of my insides, holding my pelvic bones so that I could not escape a centimeter. Miss Temple relinquished my hands and sat comfortably on the desktop, peering to get a better view of the great tumid tube as it halved me. I was going mad. I hammered

helplessly, half sobbing, on the leather desk with my poor puny fists. For it was happening again.

"NOOOOO!" I wailed hysterically. "I . . . I . . . it's toooo . . . *comeeeeeeng!*"

Great shuddering gusts of the rapture overtook me as my feet beat on his and my bucking body rooted itself greedily in the anguish of ecstasy once more.

It did not stop. I heard his gruff laugh, then—"I'm getting deeper now," and then I purely panicked. Glossy with sweat, lithe as an eel, I somehow escaped his grasp. The plug pulled out of me with a plop and I ran heedlessly . . . somewhere . . . anywhere, so be it away from him.

I got no more than yards. I remember hearing his easy, manly laugh and then that sound like a parting of curtains behind me. Swung with a full-bloodied aim, as hard as a strong man could, the last two feet of his cane caught me clean across the center of my bounding arse. It was a perfectly timed stroke and to this day I still think it one of the worst I ever had. As it clipped in, smacking upwards, I screeched soundlessly, driven out of my skin by the sting. A-tiptoe I grabbed back at my buns, never having felt such pain and knowing it was going to mount. As it did, I staggered, no more, and half-fell over a soft chair back. He got in two more ferocious swipes to the back of my thighs, the second of which made me double up whining, falling over into the chair. I huddled like a ball, holding myself, cold with pain. Heavens, what strokes he had struck me!

Miss Temple was urging me up, bending over and tugging at me. I resisted weakly, gasping and grimaced. Suddenly I felt her jolt and stiffen, a look of

startled surprise came over her face, as she called out "Oh!"

Vaguely, all I realized was that the *whup* of the rod had this time not met me. It had connected instead with the Head's bent broadside. She got one more juicy beauty there too, which made her straighten and say primly, "Broughton, please. Not before a pupil."

I was indeed somewhat aghast at the *lésé-majesté* but had little time for such reflections as now the Reverend was standing over me glowering, his wet prick purple.

"Get over that desk, girl," he grated, "quick. Or I'll cut ye to such pulp and peelings you'll wish you'd never been born."

I pantingly obeyed. En route he gave me one more furious cut with all his stinging skill. I squealed like a pig. In a trice I was re-skewered and this time he held my thighs to the desk with all the iron in his.

The pain in my cubs was so appalling I could not for a while feel anything. But when it subsided I noted a change in the monster in my belly. It was bloating as it drove into me. In panic I looked up at Miss Temple who had resumed her seat atop the desk, holding a titty of mine in her left hand while the other ruminatively rubbed the stretched velvet on her right buttock. I looked at her imploringly. *The prick was growing bigger!*

"Christ, she's tight!"

"Oh sir . . . nnnngh. . . . sir!"

"You're going to get it now, girl."

I had felt the first seething at the root. The whole thing seemed to tensen till I nearly shrieked. It was beginning to boil, engorging itself with sperm to be

spurted into me. I tried vainly to crawl forward off it. At the same time the strokes behind were now a warm gluteal glow and I could feel myself squeezing, clam-like, inside, powerless to stop the single cunt that I was from surging over with him, too, even had I wanted to, which I did not.

The root thickened, the head kicked. I heard him growl something at Miss Temple. I balanced myself up on my arms.

"Ah sir, come soon. I am giving it to you again . . . *ugggghr!*"

I jammed back on him as the spasm took me and screamed, fighting backwards, as he slowly withdrew the pole. He nodded at the entrance, once, twice, then with a great shout of "There!" he slammed full home and more in me.

"AAAAAIEEEEEE!"

As the first volt of gismic lightning was unleashed within my guts, I felt his semen travel through my marrow. What a jet! Oo, oh *ow!* The piston started pumping in single, terrific throbs, well spaced-out, each shooting thick hot gobs against me. Once, twice, thrice . . . I bit my lips and stared unseeing at Miss Temple. The throbs turned into strong upwards kicks in my belly, each thrash of sperm shaking my head on my shoulders like a ball. Would he never be done? He hosed the spew into me, until I slumped, unconscious.

When I recovered my senses the first thing I noticed was that the great glib tube within me had scarcely limpened. I still had the sensation of being thoroughly, hopelessly, filled and stuffed inside, as well as extremely sloshy from his spermatozoa. Miss Temple was talking in the skies above me.

"But Broughton, it isn't fair . . . your last visit . . . I've never had to, twice in a term like this. . . ."

"Nonsense, m'dear," came the Reverend's manly rejoinder "Do you a world of good. You know my motto: a mistress should be prepared to receive all she gives. And more."

"Besides, I think I've got the curse coming on."

"Capital. 'Twill bring it out. You've a nice round bottom and . . . but hello, what have we here? I do declare our little stranded fish has come alive again. Pour me another glass of port, do."

"Sir . . . sir!"

As I rose weakly on my arms he stiffened sullenly inside me and a mermaid at my depths began to swim to the surface at his first probing reams.

"Jove! Never met such a gluttonous cunt; you beat yer Aunt Reed, I'll swear. Now. Let's see how you like it up your bunghole. Fetch me a dollop of saddle grease, dear. . . ."

"NOOOOOH!"

"Not virgin here, I'll bet. Not if I know that Jack Reed."

He slucked juicily out of me, my cunt peeling off the fat cylinder of gristle, and presented its enormous head between my bum-cheeks. Our Headmistress anointed the sphincter ring there and then he had to vise my thighs to the desk-top in earnest, as the wet nose nuzzled for entry into my rectum. Heavens, how I fought! Again I hammered on the desk in a fury of impotence as his strong thumbs divided my puckered purse and he adroitly lodged the head, on which the sphincter closed like a clam.

"Nouuu . . . I . . . uingh!"

It had begun sliding in. He put his powerful hands

through under my armpits and caught them together at the back of my neck. I could only flail like a wounded bird, trying to climb off the impalement slowly entering into me.

"Ner-n-no more," I wailed. "No more, sir, please . . . *it won't go in!*"

"Oh yes it will," I heard in a voice very close to me now. "You'll take every inch, till you feel my balls banging into that hungry little cunt of yours, monkey. There, there. I'm going to give you something that'll make you want to shit for a week."

I slid down on the meaty shank, gulping and aghast. Finally it was all in me, a feat that made Miss Temple clap. Then she seated herself askew the desk and proceeded to toy with my button. I responded at once, grimacing.

Mr. Brocklehurst buggered me as I had never been before. It made John Reed's efforts seem like those of a pencil put in me. The man gave me the full length and girth of his member, in and out for minutes on end.

"Get ready for it," he gritted, and when he came he shot in spurts that barely let me breathe. My eyeballs bulged, my face went purple, while my traitor on Miss Temple's finger spent its grateful dew. On and on he squirted. At last I was let go. I remember falling to the floor, leaking behind in long strings, and Miss Temple consoling me there with a glass of brandy that I drank thirstily, like water. The room was beginning to spin, in any case.

"Now you've been done, Jane, wasn't it nice? Neil will see you back after she has washed you clean inside first."

"The ber-buggering was terrible," I said, lost.

"Only rather nice at the end, eh? You were most copious and I shall be grateful to you later for having reduced that stallion of his a little. Unfortunately," and her eyes strayed, "I'm afraid he means to scratch my own back a little first. I'd pull yourself to pieces, Jane, and get out of here before he sees that cane. When he's not fucking or buggering, that man likes to whip."

It was all too true. And the above was how he plucked my personal cherry at Lowood.

Yet the institution did not leave matters at that. Far from it. On entry into the Senior class each girl had to undergo a series of tests in sexual expertise, under the supervision of mistresses. These sometimes lasted over a week, one especially designated for the task.

Usually two or three mistresses (for whom this was rare sport) took as many girls through the hoops in a group. A remarkably realistic godemiche was produced and we had to show that we could lick cock, suck, and chew to the manner born. A mistress then strapped on the dildo and we were royally rammed in every conceivable position, some of which were inconceivable. We had to show that we thoroughly enjoyed it, too.

No great problem for me. I was skewered by Scottish Miss Smith and she had me paroxysming all the time. What completed the initiation was less pleasant, however. It was good deep buggery by the dildo and many girls there were that did not like it. Thanks to my early training by hateful "Master" Reed I passed with honors, easily simulating the required pleasure during the procedure, screwing back my arse and oohing and aahing as if with rapture. I am pleased to say I was applauded by our little group

when it was over. But poor Joan Walker, still thin and frail, created a frightful fuss. Oakes had on the dildo (with Hall and Seale in attendance) and despite all their efforts it could not be forced into the curiously dark anal mushroom of the half-crazed, imploring girl. She verily seemed to be able to frown with her sphincter, each time the godé was approached to the rosette. Finally, she was sentenced to what was called Blinding the Cyclops. This was extremely unpleasant and took place in a Chastisement Chamber. The girl and I who had "passed" the test first were allowed the privilege of watching.

Weeping and begging in the most piteous manner imaginable, Joan was strapped to a short leathern bench or block on her knees, which were wide parted. The bench had a curve in it which forced the back to arch, thus thrusting up and out the bottom. She was of course completely bare and her arms secured at the sides. In this obscene pose she was given four of the customarily lancinating Lowood class cuts with a thin cane by each of the presiding mistresses. Joan took this dozen with remarkable fortitude . . . but when the dread engine was approached by Miss Oakes she burst into violent tears again, writhing and squirming her bum.

But there was no defense in view, A square black wooden box was brought forward and set between the cringing buttock cheeks; from it protruded quite the most alarming imitation phallus, ebon in hue, that I have ever seen. It was not only its great girth but also the thickly and realistically ridged corona that impressed me. Mr. Brocklehurst's was no better, while the root of the thing was gnarled as some southern olive tree.

Ugh! I shuddered as it was greased and a reservoir in the box filled with a hot liquid of a milky hue but the consistency of porridge. For the monster could be made to jet.

Joan wailed as the meatus was entered into her with a thump, the box being secured to a device protruding from the bench between the legs. When fully home, it was activated by a mechanism and the Cyclops eye was fairly blinded by the plunger. This relentless and dreadfully cruel buggery tore screams from the girl at once. It was in fact much worse than the human variety, since so mechanical and unresting. The greased tube lunged forward, then withdrew slowly. Thump—out. Thump—out. Such was the rhythm and it amused the mistresses amazingly to see the thin girl so skewered. The sphincter ring clamped the monstrous engine, which plugged it quite utterly, and as it withdrew came out in a ring of whitish gut. The girl was supposed to smile and show delight to pass the test, but could not do so. She was finally released, sobbing hectically, to try again in couple of days' time, when she was promised even longer at the machine.

These were the things which vexed and were supposed to cure us at Lowood. There were many many more. Punishment Gym was one of the worst. But I have space to dilate on but one. This was Detention and since I have mentioned it in previous pages, I shall expatiate on it in those that follow, in the hope of showing how children were misused in those days long ago. It was one of our most dreaded sentences and it is only with a shudder that I set myself to limbing what happened during it here, for my reader.

Phhhh-wrlpp!

TWELVE!

As the last, and worst, of my count slogged into my writhing underbum, I jerked on my frame like some gaffed trout trying to shriek but making no sound.

What a frightful flogging. How thoroughly had it penetrated my every fiber and overcome me. I was in the German term "hewed." Every pore of me exuded pain; every inch of my flesh seemed to ache from the ministrations of that merciless ivory cane.

As I rocked in my bonds I heard him moving behind me; there was the sound of removed clothing, falling to the floor. Then that sonorous voice close up behind me, almost in my ear: "Jane, you certainly look as if you felt warm. Well—so do I!"

It was my master . . . Edward Fairfax Rochester.

12

When a girl was awarded Detention at Lowood, her name went up on a board at noon and she presented herself that day, at three o'clock in the afternoon, to the Duty Room. The award was usually for one hour or, in extremely unlucky cases, two; if three or more were awarded, they were paid off successively. On certain occasions it was possible to amnesty oneself off an hour's Detention by application to the Duty

Mistress before lunch; she might then exchange this Demerit for a tight six of the best, but it was up to the mistress to decide. Generally, since they had to be on duty through the afternoon, they liked to have three or four girls to torment—as who did not at Lowood? But the best would be for me to describe, without further preamble, my own first Detention—as a typical sample. It was to be the first of many. Three girls in all were up that afternoon: a Major called Bunty Tree, a really hefty brunette of the name of Priscilla Stevens, and humble me. Scotch Miss Smith was the presiding Duty Mistress.

"Just so long as she doesn't get out that beastly barrel," said experienced Bunty Tree as we waited disconsolately in the corridor outside the Duty Room. "I hate that."

"What I can't stand is the carrot," Priscilla opined. "Ugh! It goes so horribly deep."

I had learnt of the latter and was about to inquire of the former, when we silenced as one; steps were approaching and presently Miss Smith appeared, carrying the customary swishy cane and followed by two mischievously grinning tall maids. We dropped into curtseys, they went inside, and we waited dolefully, listening to their laughter. Then the door was thrown open and Miss Smith beckoned us in, smiling, "Come on in and make yourselves comfortable. Take all your clothes off except your shoes and stockings, and put your knickers in that barrel over there."

The first thing I saw was a polished wood water barrel; the second was a rank of three frightful "carrots," of which I had heard Aunt Reed referring to Mr. Brocklehurst. We shivered as we stripped, the maids occupying themselves with dismaying prepara-

tives at the side and the mistress swinging her stick.

It was said that much of the ritual of Detention had gone by the day I got to Lowood. There had been an infamous Black Box, it seemed, and certain chips of wood, and frightful shoes with spikes under the heels in which you had to walk. Perhaps some of the apparatus had passed into disuse; there was still enough to vex us horribly—thin jets of scalding water, and methods of suspension that were ingenious and ignoble in the extreme. Detention was meant to be a deterrent, and was.

When we were ready, Miss Smith called our names and announced an hour for each. Then she said briskly, "Stand out, Bunty, and bend over with your palms on the ground."

Bunty Tree duly received five whistlers, right in the fold, then Priscilla four, myself three. While we stood rubbing ourselves, Miss Smith said, "Now then. I advise you three to co-operate wholeheartedly. If you do not I shall have no hesitation in awarding you a Demerit and helping you to pay it off tonight, over the board. You are not here to enjoy yourselves and we shall begin by seeing how you like sitting on one of our special stools for a matter of twenty minutes or so. Rose, Catherine," she called to the maids, "are all the carrots eight inches?"

"Or more, Miss."

"Put them on, then."

We approached the three stools, ranged one behind the other, most gloomily. Their purpose was all too plain, even if we had not known it, from hearsay, already. Each stool was more a saddle than such, low and with its wooden seat flanged out to separate the hinds. From the center reared up obscenely a

thick black meatus or prick, already coated with grease by the maids. These monstrous dildoes with their bloated heads had but one errand—to go up us, deep.

Bunty Tree straddled her carrot first, thoughtfully. Before she lowered herself on it her wrists were secured high up her back behind (a woman's can go much higher than a man's) and the shackle secured to a bit between her teeth, which held her head well back. Then she squatted slowly, each maid holding wide her hams. The dildo divided her, sinking slowly up her gut; suddenly, when it seemed half up, the maids yanked at her ankles and with a grunted cry she impaled herself helplessly on the thick false prick. Her ankles were then fastened under the stool so that no purchase on the floor was possible. The girl was potently pierced. It was the turn of big Priscilla Stevens.

Poor Priscilla made a frightful fuss, begging off piteously until well and truly bitted. Her great blubbery buttocks were quivering like those of some mare in heat as she lowered herself, squatting. The cobra knob entered the anal dimple, grotesquely distending it, then she uttered a shrill squeak as the malicious maids yanked back her ankles and visibly, before my aghast eyes, the girl's weight slowly impaled her on the greasy pole to its very root. Her buttock cheeks squashed sideways on the twin wings of the stool and, with knees parted, her ankles too were brought back and secured beneath the frightful seat. My turn was next.

"Big enough for you, Jane? I think you'll feel you've got something up you in a moment. Count yourself lucky it's greased."

The edges of my lips were now being treated to a little of the same crude oil—preparatory to the biting —for they were not cruel at Lowood.

"Right down on it now."

My legs were astraddle the awful thing. I began to squat, distaste writ large on my writhen features. Though my head was back, I could just see in front of me the broad fat back of my predecessor; sweat was slipping down the furrow deeply drawn between her shoulder-blades and she was making hopeless efforts to wriggle up off the cruel skewer dividing her. Then the cold knob prodded at me. Ah God! The head slipped in, the thick corona popping into the ring of muscle there, and then the wicked maids caught me up under each buttock cheek, holding my legs behind the knees. I knew what they were going to do and squirmed lustily, legs off the ground entirely, and impaling myself more in the process. They let me have a good long slide down the dreadful dong and by the time they had secured my ankles beneath me, it was splitting me in two.

How would you, gentle reader, care to sit for twenty minutes in this pose, with a stout plug up your guts? I thought it a rotten way to treat a girl, and still do. Our breathing came fast, our lips drooled; Priscilla was making a regular snoring sound in front of me. After what seemed a century Miss Smith said cheerily, "You have had one minute, girls."

My seat was soon slippery with sweat; the more one tried to squeeze up off it, the more soundly did one seem to impale oneself on the "carrot." I had a constant feeling of wanting to "go." We were all

breathing like runners when the mistress said quietly, "Increase penetration. One inch."

Mad groans of protest from Priscilla. It was done, by some mechanism beneath the seats. And it was done once more before we were finished. Finally, to our terror, the command was given to the maids to rotate the things within us. The great fisted heads started to revolve within our depths. Then the groans of the damned truly began. Never had I known such griping. A cold sweat broke out on my forehead; a steam arose before my eyes. The rotation was slow but solid, probing to the depths of our clenching intestines. At last the smiling face of the Scotch mistress with the red hair appeared in the mists above me and I realized I was being raised by the two maids. I arose shakily, to the accompaniment of a long suctioning sound completed by a loud pop. I fell on my side on the floor somewhere, bumping my head into Priscilla's base there; it was a softish bump. We all lay panting, our sweaty flesh heaving, still cruelly bitted and bound, while the next atrocity was prepared for us.

For there was never any respite in Detention. Up it was—the creamy fat before me streaked with two blue lines for slowness in rising—and over to the celebrated "bar."

From another wall, at about chest-height, protruded a number of ebony rails, each about as long as a stout walking stick and no thicker than it; each was serrated or notched atop, and grease had been put here too. We were allotted fifteen minutes astride these fiendish seats, being mounted in turn.

Facing the wall, still bitted and bound, I had to

stand on two stools either side the bar and stride it. Then I must lower the most tender portion of my anatomy and take my horrid "seat." A maid made sure one's lips were well parted and that the bar sank fully in each vulnerable vulva. We hung thus helplessly, our legs each side, as the stools were taken away. Finally, a rod was extended from the wall which pushed back our shins; in this way the seat was made more cruel than ever. We were hinged like three parallel bows, frowning at the wall and sweating like mad; it was impossible to shift or swing one's weight in any way thus, so as to mitigate the dreadful pressure on the cunt.

I think I minded this the most, though I did hear the dull thud of a cut as Bunty Tree got a beauty for something. Though heavy, Priscilla made less protest than she had on the carrot. Each girl had her personal dislikes. Again an aeon seemed to pass, when behind us we heard, "For the last five minutes, the weights."

The shin-rods were removed and heavy weights affixed to our ankles. This was quite excruciating and I for one began to babble and shout. Judging from the sounds about me the others did so, too. All else that could be heard were the rich chuckles of the maids, watching us. When we were let down, we veritably huddled on that floor like so many slaughtered birds of prey, sides still palpitating, but that was all. There was, we surmised, one more ordeal possible in the time allotted. I prayed it would not be the high platform which, like that hoisting at Mrs. Reed's, attacked some sensitive portion of my soul.

For the final fifteen minutes—the preparations filled in the rest of the hour—we were crucially

stretched or racked. First, we redonned our corsets which were breathlessly tightly laced. Then, in line, each of us was stretched in parallel apparatuses horizontal to the floor and a few feet above it. Cuffs at ankles and wrists were hauled excruciatingly taut. I felt that my bones were being pulled out of my sockets and began to sweat again. Each of us was blindfold for this rite. The racking was such that, with the corset on, it was impossible to control a muscle of one's body anywhere. One was helpless, at the mercy of the mistress presiding. I heard my fellows groan and gasp. Smith ordered trays set beneath us.

At last, when I hoped it was over, I felt the maids parting my legs by the mechanism. When they were wide spread something was slid into my entrails. It felt softer than the dong—and then suddenly it did not. The intruder was being inflated! I began to burst, writhing. Useless to try to clench my buttocks against it—no effort of mine had any effect on my muscles there. Suddenly I panicked. Cries sounded either side of me.

"Hou!"

"Au!"

THE THING WAS BEING HEATED!

I was in a perfect frenzy of ecstasy as the heat grew within me, then suddenly the frightful snake was slipped out. Involuntarily, as from another part of myself, I felt myself empty itself, in spasmic gusts of exusion. Lusty thumps from right and left accompanied my own. Much merriment from the maids.

Miss Smith said, "Look what that Priscilla has done. 'Tis worthy of a Guardsman, I declare. Rose, do you remove the trays and Cathy, please wipe them clean."

When we were released we were bathed in sweat and no strength was left in us at all; but the worst was to come.

Thoroughly defeated, and meek as mice, we were herded at the far end of the room. The beastly barrel was at the other now. Our knickers lay within it. Miss Smith addressed us:

"You have now had an hour's Detention. Next time I shall make it stiffer. We shall conclude by a little target practice. The loser will receive ten cuts from the winner—over the board." During this ominous announcement I noticed the maids, and the mistress herself, arming themselves with short feathered darts. They looked heavy. "What is a bull's-eye, Bunty?"

"Arsehole, Miss," came the disconsolate answer.

"Right in one," returned Miss Smith warmly. "But an 'inner' can be awfully uncomfortable too. Now line up and get ready. So. In that barrel are your knickers. You ought to know your own smells by now. The winner is the first girl to get her knicks out and sit herself on a carrot again. Are you ready?" I began to realize the enormity of the thing. We were not bitted, but our hands were bound behind us. The barrel looked a long distance away. It would clearly only be possible for one girl at a time, so fettered, to insinuate her upper person over the edge and pick out the necessary morsel of material—in her teeth. As the maids readied their darts I also realized she would have to bend double to do so. Holy Mother in Heaven. Ten cuts! Three had been agony . . . oh God oh God. . . .

"GO!"

We leapt forward as one. Priscilla got ahead, but-

tocking forward heavily and shoving Bunty off stride. I saw Miss Smith make a feathering motion, something whooshed softly past me in the air, and I had time to see a dark thuck into Priscilla's bounding left buttock, crimsoning instantly as it lodged there. I had time—before I straightened with a strangled cry as a wasp bit inside my left thigh. I looked down. The dart had bounced off, leaving a stab of blood. As I stopped in terror, however, another whucked home into my braced right hind, sinking in an inch or more. The pain was unspeakable and I bounded forward with a yell. Another struck my corset and fell off harmlessly. Our three tormentors were laughing and congratulating each other as they threw. What heartlessness!

Thwuck!

"Good shot, Rose!"

A beauty drove into Bunty's left. What would happen when we b-b-bent over. . . .

Bunty and Priscilla were barging at the barrel, myself beside them watching. Sheer weight won and Priscilla plunged her torso, hands bound behind her, into the dark depths of the barrel, kicking one leg up, perhaps in some hopeless effort at protection.

Whsssh. . . whsssssh. . . . whhhhhlck!

Three darts thudded into the thick meat of her cheeks. One dropped off but the other two drove in, oozing blood at once She wriggled frantically while darts whizzed through the air, then purple in face came up with a pair of knickers in her teeth.

Rose-red! Mine!

In fury she flung them from her with a toss of her head, hoping to make it hard for me to get them while she amassed her own; but by this time Bunty

had cleverly climbed over into the barrel before her. I saw no more. I only felt. Two frightful bites inside my thighs were what I felt as I bent for my knicks and then I was racing back with them to skewer myself on a carrot. I was the winner.

Priscilla was the loser. Despite the fact that she was pitifully wealed and runneling blood behind from the dart-marks, I had to put her over the board and give her ten with Miss Smith's elastic cane. As adjunct to this first instruction in rodding, the mistress stood behind me and each time I did not cut hard enough in her estimation, she gave me a razor-slice with her switch. The big fat buttock, well bent, was a tempting spectacle indeed and I must confess I whipped it with a will. The skin seemed particularly tender low down and it was there I worked her best, extracting grievous cries by the end.

Such, then, was my first hour's Detention; like all our corrections at Lowood, it made me realize how little I was, and in need of reminding of my position.

True, reader: I am a defective being, with many faults and few redeeming points. Yet I still feel a strange sense of attachment for Lowood and never cease to cherish the memories of those first tender excitements than animated my heart, and made of pain a pleasure. Those joys I was to satisfy, later, with Mr. Rochester.

The years passed quickly, as young years do, and a kind fairy saw to it that my uniform life was relieved by rising to be the first girl of the first class.

Then I was invested with the office of teacher, of a junior sort, a task which I discharged with relish, especially when it included thrashing some blubbering girl for a nothing. For, yes, I became expert in use of the rod, chiefly under the tutelage of the French mistress, Madame Pierrot, who gave me long lessons (invariably ending in ecstasy) in application of the strokes. How assiduously did I practice my art on special bolsters and leathern horses, striving to exact the ultimate smart from each stinging stripe. No fencer ever tried harder!

Finally, however, I felt I was perfect and knew I needed freedom—freedom to indulge my long-trained, new-found fancy. I would go to be a governess and get a charge and whip her to my heart's content. Such were my silly fancies at the time.

Miss Temple it was who told me how to advertise. And lent me the money for it, too. I directed my plea to the editor of the *Herald,* put it in the post, with answers to be addressed to J.E. My advertisement ran thus:

> A young lady accustomed to tuition [had I not been so!] is desirous of meeting with a situation in a private family . . . she is qualified to teach the usual branches of a good English education, together with French, Drawing, and Music.

The succeeding week was long. Then one evening, after I had read prayers to the school, Neil brought me a letter. The seal was an initial F. I broke it. The contents were brief. If "J.E." who advertised in the *Herald* possessed the acquirements mentioned, then "a situation can be offered her where there is but one

pupil, a little girl, and where the salary is thirty pounds per annum.'

It was signed: Mrs. Fairfax, Thornfield, near Millcote, —shire.

My heart leapt and I reread the document many times, till my candle sank. Next day first steps were taken to my new mode of life. Miss Temple then laid the affair before Mr. Brocklehurst who gave me a testimonial and a final thrashing. The former was despatched to Mrs. Fairfax and the latter given me before Miss Temple. This fond farewell was, as ever, excruciatingly painful, a tight twelve "on the bare," taken touching my toes. I am glad to say that such was training by then that I suffered stoically until the last strokes, when he began to cut me about the top of the legs. I have always found this hideously painful and was forced to reward him with some sorry clasping and grimacing after. All the same I was able to put my clothes to rights without too much commotion and look him, pink-cheeked, in the eyes.

"Thank you, sir," I said and dropped him a controlled curtsey.

He flexed his cane with the nearest to a loving smile I had ever seen him give a girl.

"Well, I trust that will make you want to stand up in the coach, Jane." For my box was corded, the card nailed on, I had sought in all my drawers to see no article was left behind; and I was to be fetched from Lowood presently. "I have enjoyed flogging you, and having you flogged, and I hope it has done you good here."

"Oh it has, sir," I said warmly. Then impulsively I began, "I want to thank you—" but choked myself. What was I saying? Suddenly I heard myself, and

it was as if Eliza Reed were in that room speaking: "Oh I thank you, sir, for everything you have done for me, and especially for ravishing me and thrashing me. Yours were always the worst whippings, the most thoroughly punishing, and they did rare honor to us." Suddenly I was crying and now it was Helen Burns speaking, Helen who had left a year before for a place in Essex—"But, sir, I never had the soko from you and if you wished, if you were so very kind, I would like to offer my person to it now."

He looked at me long and steadily across his cane. Finally he said, "It will be two dozen, Jane, and there may be some stains on that black traveling dress of yours when you arrive."

"I shall never wash them out, sir."

After another long interval in which he measured me, he said, "Take up your things and lie down before me and grip my ankles. Now—BRING ME THE STRICTEST SOKO THAT WE HAVE!"

Later, sitting tingling in the coach, I knew that a phase of my life was closing, a new one opening tomorrow. Little girl, I thought to myself with a smile, may your bottom be chubby and the twigs in the trees near Millcote whippy, for I mean to give you "a good English education" with plenty of it spent eyeing the carpet from close to, arse in air. How sadly this hope was to be disillusioned I knew not then. But that is another story. . . .

END OF VOLUME ONE

Addicted
Ray Gordon

Housewife, Helen Hunter, has it all. An attractive, successful husband. Money. Looks. However, things go wrong when her husband leaves on business. She becomes tired, nervy and anxious...panicky even. But on his return—after a hearty 'welcome'—the symptoms disappear. Something bizarre is happening—she has become addicted to sperm.

The supply from her husband soon becomes insufficient. She embarks on an incredible sexual journey to satisfy her desires. Unfortunately it soon becomes apparent that too much is never enough...

Slave Girls of Rome
Don Winslow

Master eroticist Don Winslow takes an erotic look back on the Roman Empire during its ascendancy in the world. This is a tale of power and pleasure. Never has a city been as depraved as Rome—and never have women been so relentlessly used as were Rome's voluptuous slaves! With no choice but to serve their lustful masters, these captive beauties had to perform their duties with the passion and purpose of Venus herself.

Lusts of the Borgias
Marcus Van Heller

Italy, during the Renaissance, was a time of culture but also of uninhibited corruption. And no powerful family of the age was more depraved than the infamous House of Borgia. Here is the story of their cruel, passionate, erotic adventures.

> "One of the few historical erotic novels worthy of being called a classic. [It is also] a novel of outrageous sexual indulgence."
> —*Evergreen Review*

Order These Selected Blue Moon Titles

Title	Price
Souvenirs From a Boarding School	$7.95
The Captive	$7.95
Ironwood Revisited	$7.95
The She-Slaves of Cinta Vincente	$7.95
The Architecture of Desire	$7.95
The Captive II	$7.95
Shadow Lane	$7.95
Services Rendered	$7.95
Shadow Lane III	$7.95
My Secret Life	$9.95
The Eye of the Intruder	$7.95
Net of Sex	$7.95
Captive V	$7.95
Cocktails	$7.95
Girl School	$7.95
The New Story of O	$7.95
Shadow Lane IV	$7.95
Beauty in the Birch	$7.95
The Blue Train	$7.95
Wild Tattoo	$7.95
Ironwood Continued	$7.95
Transfer Point Nice	$7.95
Souvenirs from a Boarding School	$7.95
Secret Talents	$7.95
Shadow Lane V	$7.95
Bizarre Voyage	$7.95
Red Hot	$7.95
Images of Ironwood	$7.95
Tokyo Story	$7.95
The Comfort of Women	$7.95
Disciplining Jane	$7.95
The Passionate Prisoners	$7.95
Doctor Sex	$7.95
Shadow Lane VI	$7.95
Girl's Reformatory	$7.95
The City of One-Night Stands	$7.95
A Hunger in Her Flesh	$7.95
Flesh On Fire	$7.95
Hard Drive	$7.95
Secret Talents	$7.95
The Captive's Journey	$7.95
Elena Raw	$7.95
La Vie Parisienne	$7.95
Fetish Girl	$7.95
Road Babe	$7.95
Violetta	$7.95
Story of O	$5.95
Dark Matter	$7.95
Ironwood	$7.95
Body Job	$7.95
Arousal	$7.95
The Blue Moon Erotic Reader II	$15.95

Visit our website at www.bluemoonbooks.com